Summer's Flame

I0674177

Wendy Davy

Summer's Flame
COPYRIGHT 2015 by Wendy Davy

All scripture quotations, unless otherwise indicated, are taken from the Holy Bible, New International Version®, NIV®. Copyright 1973, 1978, 1984, 2011 by Biblica, Inc.™ Used by permission of Zondervan. All rights reserved worldwide. www.zondervan.com

Cover Art by *Nicola Martinez*

White Rose Publishing, a division of Pelican Ventures, LLC
www.pelicanbookgroup.com PO Box 1738 *Aztec, NM * 87410
White Rose Publishing Circle and Rosebud logo is a trademark of Pelican Ventures, LLC

Food for the Poor® is a trademark of Food for the Poor, Inc. Use of the Food for the Poor® trademark is not an endorsement by Food for the Poor, Inc. of Pelican Ventures, LLC; this book; or any of the concepts found within its pages.

Publishing History
First White Rose Edition, 2015
978-1-61116-508-1 Electronic
978-1-61116-509-8 Paperback
Published in the United States of America

Dedication

Dedicated to the glory of God.
Special thanks to Debbie and Kathy for sharing your
beloved pets with my characters, and to Laura and
Bruce for sharing your expertise.

About the Author

Wendy Davy is an award-winning, inspirational romance author with several titles available. She uses her active imagination and love of adventure to create faith-based stories of the heart. When not writing, she spends time reading, enjoying her real-life hero, and watching movies. She loves hearing from her readers and can be contacted at wendy@wendydavy.com.

What People Are Saying

Deadly Chase ~ 2013 Inspirational Reader's Choice Award Finalist and The Romance Reviews Top Pick:

"*Deadly Chase* was filled with suspense as well as sweet, blissful romance. The chemistry between the two characters was amazing. If you love reading a good romance story with a twist of suspense, then this book is for you." ~ CozyReader, The Romance Reviews

Reluctant Bridesmaid ~ 1st Place Winner in the 2010 San Antonio Romance Authors Merritt Contest and Night Owl Reviews Top Pick:

"*Reluctant Bridesmaid* by Wendy Davy is a charming romance with likable characters and lively dialogue. While the growing romance between Jordan and Tanner is the main focus of the story, the author also focuses on their Christian faith and how the events in their lives have shaped their beliefs and their willingness to depend on God to get them through their troubles." ~ Maria, Night Owl Reviews

You Can't Hide

"*You Can't Hide* had me hooked from the very beginning and didn't let me go until the last page was turned. It was like watching an intense movie where you find yourself wringing your hands and taking quick breaths." ~ Sherry, Love 2 Read Novels

"There is no fear in love.
But perfect love drives out fear."
~ 1 John 4:18

1

Summer Cassel plunged the paddle into the water, battling Shenandoah River's powerful current. The recreational kayak sliced across the rippling surface, forging ahead as if it were as eager as Summer to reach the wild blackberry brambles. The plump, ripe fruit would make a delicious cobbler, and she could use the dessert as a catalyst to initiate conversation with the elusive neighbor who had moved into her apartment complex three weeks ago.

With only five units comprising the renovated historic hotel tucked in Virginia's countryside, an official welcoming committee didn't exist, so Summer had taken it upon herself to make Mr. Hawk feel at home at The Meadows, even though she had yet to properly introduce herself. Of course, that wasn't her fault. He'd skirted around her each time they'd crossed paths as if she carried some kind of contagious disease. The only reason she knew the attractive, dark-haired man's name was because of the engraved label her landlord had placed on Mr. Hawk's mailbox. She was sure a fresh, warm blackberry cobbler would open the door to conversation.

But first, she had to harvest the main ingredient.

As she continued her steady strokes, nature invited her into its folds. Thick woodlands masked Summer from sparse homesteads located alongside the river, and blocked the view of the nearby Blue Ridge Mountains. She'd think herself alone in the wilderness, if not for the occasional group of adventure seekers passing by on inner tubes or canoes.

Although the early June temperatures rose to uncomfortable levels, sycamore, river birch, and silver maple trees stretched over the winding waterway, creating ample shade—a true blessing in the midafternoon heat.

Scents of ripe fruit caught on the breeze. Summer scanned the shoreline and found her target, exactly where her landlord had described: after the second bend in the river, ten feet to the left of a towering cypress tree. The brambles stretched above overgrown grass, a mass of thorny tangles overflowing with nourishing fruit.

The river's strong current and rocky terrain made maneuvering to the riverbank a concentrated effort. After avoiding numerous underwater obstacles, Summer managed to beach the kayak and secure a rope to a small tree. She climbed across exposed root systems and fallen branches, and by the time she reached the blackberries, beads of perspiration trickled down her chest and back, soaking her favorite tank top. But it didn't matter. She was about to get her hands dirty, her arms scratched, and expose herself to ticks and various insects. A little sweat was the least of her worries.

She only hoped Aiden Hawk would appreciate her efforts.

Summer plucked a blackberry from the vine and sampled it. Sweet. Ripe. Perfect for her needs. Anticipation fluttered in her belly. She could taste the cobbler already.

One hour and many thorn pricks later, Summer had an overflowing bucket. She returned to the kayak, secured the blackberries, and then shoved away from shore. Using the paddle to steer, she allowed the swift current to carry her toward home as she considered her plan.

Mr. Hawk kept odd hours. Sometimes he would disappear for days at a time, but she hoped he'd be in at some point this evening. She only knew of his unconventional routine, of course, because she'd been trying to speak with him and not because stirrings of attraction swamped her each time she caught a glimpse of his tall frame and athletic build. Not to mention his unruly dark hair, his square jaw, and his deep blue eyes...

So, she wasn't immune to a good-looking guy. Big deal. She was human.

Regardless of his appeal, this upcoming meet and greet was strictly about making proper introductions and welcoming him to the building—same as she'd done in the past with other new tenants. He was her neighbor, after all. With his door directly across the hall from hers, they were bound to run into each other from time to time. And it would be awkward if they didn't speak.

Summer made certain the bucket of berries remained steady, and then aimed the kayak toward the river's center as she neared a set of Class II rapids. The fun stretch had her bobbing along for a few minutes until she reached calm waters again.

As snatches of The Meadows came into view, Summer marveled at how well her landlord, Frank Hamilton, had transformed the 1930s hotel into a sleek and modern apartment complex. From the outside, the two-story stone and wood structure looked like a charming cottage complete with a well-maintained wraparound porch. But it was the inside that had solidified Summer's decision to sign the lease and move in last year. She loved the apartment's open floor plan, the French doors leading to a private balcony overlooking the river, and the living room's wood-beamed cathedral ceilings. The place felt like home the moment she'd stepped in the door.

The air conditioning worked great, too. Which reminded her...she was hot, thirsty, her scratches stung, and the perspiration she hadn't minded a while ago had begun to make her skin itch. She swiped aside a rolling sweat bead and paddled toward shore.

It would've been nice if along with all the reconstruction, Frank could've put in a boat ramp beside the dock. When she'd suggested it, he had informed her it was a choice between having hot water heaters in the apartments or a ramp. She liked having hot water. He'd made the right decision.

So, here she was with a nine-foot kayak and a steep shoreline over which she had to haul it. She'd done so before, many times, but each time, she was sure she would pull a muscle. Oh well, steep bank or not, she would accomplish her mission.

The kayak bumped against the shore, and Summer stepped into the cool water. Carefully, she set the bucket of blackberries on land first, then grabbed the kayak and tugged it toward the crest of the hill where the beach met the grass. The boat slid several inches and teetered on the edge. One more pull should suffice.

Familiar rumblings of a truck pulling into the parking lot at The Meadows broke her concentration. Aiden Hawk drove a black, full-sized, double-cab pick-up, and the powerful engine liked to make an announcement each time it arrived.

Summer pictured herself from Mr. Hawk's point of view. She must look a sight with her hair in disarray, her arms stretched to their limits, and her damp clothes plastered to her body. Maybe he would continue inside without giving her a second look, or even a first one.

She spared a glance over her shoulder. No such luck.

His blue-eyed gaze was trained on her. He took a step toward her, concern marring his brow.

Her stomach sank. If he got too close now, she'd scare him away for certain. She needed to get cleaned up before he came within a ten-foot radius. With renewed determination, Summer put every ounce of strength into one last yank. The boat gave way, plopping onto the grass as she fell backward.

Mr. Hawk stilled, waiting as if unsure what to do.

Summer gave a thumbs-up, hoping he'd do what he always did—disappear into The Meadows and make a beeline for his apartment. If he'd only waited a few more minutes to come home, she could've introduced herself properly.

Oh well. Nothing she could do about that now.

"I'm all right." Summer climbed to her knees. "I've got everything under control."

His concerned expression eased, and he ducked his head and busied himself with something inside his vehicle.

Summer relaxed. His touch of concern was nice, but she really would've been embarrassed to have him come too close.

Dottie Carlson emerged from the apartment complex with Patches, her beloved Chihuahua, tucked in her arms. She waved at Aiden Hawk and shuffled toward Summer, her white hair bouncing in the breeze. As Dottie crossed the well-manicured lawn, Patches grew anxious and wiggled out of her arms. He landed with legs already pumping, gaze zeroed in on Summer. Like a slingshot, he surged forward, leaving tufts of grass flying in his wake.

She'd been targeted.

Should've known better than to give him bits of her steak dinner the last time she'd watched him for Dottie. Now, Patches was forever her best friend, with all the rewards.

Summer braced herself, but one could only do so much in preparation for dog kisses.

With less than a yard to spare, Patches leapt into the air and landed on her chest. The eight-pound, rock-solid canine knocked her backward. This was no ordinary Chihuahua. Eager to please and full of affection, Patches licked Summer's face.

"Patches. Mind your manners," Dottie admonished, but a smile adorned her wrinkled features.

"It's OK." Summer wrapped her arms around him and accepted the greeting. In the condition she was in, what harm could a little dog spittle do? She laughed as Patches continued to welcome her home as if she'd been gone for weeks.

"You've been feeding him people food again, haven't you?" Dottie's hands found her ample hips.

"Who, me?" She feigned innocence. "Maybe a little. Besides, you never said he couldn't have leftovers."

Dottie's smile widened. "Well, he's all I have left to spoil. Might as well do it right."

Summer eased Patches from her lap and stood. She attempted to brush the fur off her tank top, but errant strands stuck to the damp material and added to her already unkempt appearance.

Self-conscious, Summer allowed her gaze to stray toward the parking lot.

Aiden Hawk stood alongside his truck, looking her way. His features relaxed with a grin.

Then, their gazes met.

He straightened, tucked hands into pockets, and then turned and hurried into the building. But not before she caught sight of the pink staining his cheeks. Or had she imagined his reaction? A strong, virile man like that wouldn't blush. She must be seeing things.

Shaking her head, Summer took up the kayak's rope, dragged the boat into the storage shed and secured the door. Dusting her hands, she returned her attention to Dottie. "I'm making a cobbler to welcome Mr. Hawk to The Meadows."

"Oh, he will like that. He has a sweet tooth. Not that you could tell by looking at him." Dottie kept an eye on Patches and when he got too close to the water, called the dog back.

"How do you know he likes sweets? He doesn't talk."

Dottie retrieved Patches. "Aiden talks plenty. Just not to you."

"Hold on. Wait." Summer wanted answers. "What do you mean?"

Dottie ran her fingers through her dog's fur. "He's quite friendly, actually. He helps me carry groceries from the car. Holds the door open for me. You know, all the stuff gentlemen do. And in town, most all the folks know and like him."

"That's...interesting." What else could she say? Apparently, Aiden Hawk was a mystery only to her. But not for long. She scooped up the bucket of blackberries. "I'm going inside to get started on the cobbler. Did you need me to watch Patches for you tonight?" There had to be some reason Dottie had ventured into the afternoon heat.

"That would be wonderful. I'm going to Glade Springs Volunteer Fire Department for a couple rounds of bingo with Frank. You know how Patches gets lonely when I leave him for too long." Dottie tucked him closer under her arm and nuzzled his fur. "Don't you, sweetheart?"

Patches looked up with adoring eyes.

"I still say Patches isn't a Chihuahua. He's too relaxed. And loving." And Patches had never tried to nip her heels like others of the breed.

"Oh, he is a purebred, dear. He's got papers. He's just one of a kind." Dottie's love for the animal shone through her eyes and her voice. "I'll bring him to your apartment." She checked her watch. "In about an hour. If that's OK?"

"That's fine. That'll give me time to take a shower and make the cobbler." Summer headed toward the building as a sense of urgency mounted. If she had any hopes of officially meeting Aiden Hawk, she had to do it quick before he disappeared again.

~*~

Aiden rushed into his apartment, turned, and placed both hands on the mahogany door, slamming it shut. Resting his forehead against the cool wood, he contemplated knocking some sense into his own brain. What was he thinking? He'd been presented with yet another opportunity—probably the best one yet—to meet the beautiful woman residing in apartment 2A, and he'd blown it.

He shouldn't have hesitated. He'd known she could handle the kayak from seeing her use it before, but he'd been close enough to help her this time. Why hadn't he stepped forward as he would've with any other woman wrestling a heavy load?

Because she wasn't any other woman. She was Summer Cassel.

The sweet-looking, doe-eyed brunette had flustered him from the first moment he'd laid eyes on her. If only he could approach her as he did a burning building—with confidence and unyielding determination. But no, a sudden shy streak had blindsided him, claiming his common sense. He should've introduced himself from the beginning. Now their chance encounters were becoming awkward.

Today, with Dottie standing alongside Summer as a buffer, he could've come up with any number of things to say to either or both of them. The weather had been great. He could've talked about that. Then again, talking about the weather in summer—*to* Summer—would've been a disaster. It was probably better that his face had heated with a blush, making him turn away and saving him from an even more embarrassing encounter.

The guys at the station would get such a kick out of this if they ever found out about it. He'd told only one person about his interest in his neighbor. Captain Warren knew all the specifics. Aiden trusted the man with his life. Of course, he trusted the other firefighters with his life, too. But Captain Warren was the only one Aiden trusted with his secrets.

He shook his head and ran a hand down his face as his thoughts continued to wander. Most of the men and women he worked alongside had families. Children. Spouses. Summer's image came to mind.

"Yeah, keep dreaming," he chastised himself, his musings echoing across the hardwood floor. He'd have to get an area rug. He was tired of the empty sounds. Although he'd fully furnished the place, it still seemed too big for one person. Spending his time helping others in need had once been enough, but lately...nothing filled the growing ache in his soul.

Aiden sighed, strode across the room, and opened the French doors leading onto the balcony. Fresh air was what he needed. And if Summer was still outside, maybe he could work up the courage to offer a hello. An initial greeting from the second story wasn't ideal, but at least it was something. Each day that passed without speaking to her became a missed opportunity. He stepped onto the wide balcony, scanned the yard below. She was gone.

Disappointment and a little bit of relief flowed. The mixed emotions wore on him. He really needed to get this over with or risk forming a stomach ulcer.

Before he could think it through and change his mind, he re-entered his apartment, yanked open his front door, and forced his legs to carry him across the hall to apartment 2A. Fisting his hand, he knocked three times.

The resounding thumps mirrored his thundering

heart. Seconds passed as he stared at the solid wood door. No noises of any kind seeped through. No shadow passed on the other side of the peephole. The paneled door stayed shut.

Summer might have gone out. But her small blue SUV was still parked in the driveway.

Most likely, she was avoiding him. At this point, he wouldn't blame her. More than once, he'd treated her like she had cooties. And the time he'd ducked back into his apartment as she'd come out of her door, well, that was just sad. He hadn't meant to be unfriendly. He'd panicked.

But he wouldn't this time. He gathered his courage, knocked on the door again, and waited.

Nothing happened.

Great. Now he'd have to work up the nerve again some other time. Raking fingers through his hair, he once again sought the solace of his apartment.

2

Summer stepped out of the shower, picked up a towel, and dried off. Human again, she set about getting dressed. She'd been told the fitted lavender sundress complemented her eyes, so after deliberating between three outfits, she chose the dress.

She carefully applied makeup, dried her hair, and then glanced in the mirror, turning one way and then the next. The rigorous kayaking trips she'd been taking had paid off. The ten pounds she'd lost in the past few months had given her a trim waistline, and she loved the look. Now, if she could gather the courage to donate the clothes that were now too big for her...

She eyed the jeans she had placed on the shelf, up high and out of the way. One day she'd let go of them, but for now, she'd play it safe and keep them. There were some risks she wasn't yet ready to take. Summer paused. Who was she kidding? She didn't take risks at all, and she liked it that way. Less chance of getting hurt.

Summer headed for the kitchen. The clock on the microwave showed she'd spent forty minutes getting cleaned up. Her heart skipped a beat. If she didn't hurry, Aiden Hawk could complete another vanishing act.

Rushing, she plunked the blackberries into a colander, rinsed them with cold water, and set them aside to drain. Next, she dug in the cabinet for sugar. But how much was she supposed to use? One cup or two? And the butter? A half stick or a whole? She didn't want to take a chance, so she shuffled through a drawer for her recipe.

Sifting past masking tape, screwdrivers, and old coupons, Summer made a mental note to organize her things soon. Finally, she gave up.

She retrieved her cellphone and brought up Riley's number. By the time her sister answered, Summer's tension had skyrocketed. "Riley, it's me. I figured out a way to finally meet that neighbor I've been telling you about, Aiden Hawk. He's home tonight. Or at least I think he still is. I need Grandma's cobbler recipe ASAP before he takes off again." She set the sugar on the granite countertop.

"I need a lot of things, too." Riley's voice came across clear and precise. "My car wouldn't start this morning. Zack got caught stealing from the convenience store again, and my boss says if I don't go on the next business trip, I'll be fired."

Well, that put things into perspective. Guilt stung, as it always did when it came to Riley. "I'm sorry."

Riley let out a long sigh. "No. I'm sorry. I didn't mean to download my problems on you. I'm . . . handling things." Handling things was what Riley did best. As a recent widow and a single mother to a teenager, she had no other choice.

"If you need me, I can come back and live with you again. Just say the word."

"You spent six months with us. I couldn't ask you to give up more of your life. Besides, Zack and I have to find our new normal. We have to figure out how to be a family again."

A family without a father. Without a husband. Summer understood Riley's unspoken words.

"I accepted the risks when I married a police officer. I knew that one day he might not come home." Riley's voice broke.

Summer remembered the details. She was there when Riley received the news that her husband had been killed in the line of duty, and Summer was there in the months afterward helping Riley piece her life back together.

Neither one of them walked away the same.

Riley had been shaken to her core. And as a witness to the devastation, Summer had vowed to never become involved with a man in a dangerous profession. But she hadn't called Riley to delve into painful circumstances. She'd simply wanted a recipe. Summer searched for a way to change the subject but came up blank. As the silence stretched, Summer's tension grew. "Is there anything I can do?"

"Pray for us."

"I do. Every day." Summer opened the sugar and a few fine grains fell onto the counter. "If you don't have the recipe, it's OK. I'll just—"

"You're not the type to wing it." Riley's tone softened. "You're a good cook, Summer. But not that good." Leave it to Riley to speak with brutal honesty.

Summer didn't mind. She'd rather have the truth than meaningless words. "I know. Thanks for reminding me."

"I can't get to my recipes right now, but I made a cobbler not too long ago. I remember what I used." Riley rattled off the ingredients and measurements. "Be sure to cook it until it's golden brown on the edges."

"Thanks. I owe you one."

"Let me know how it goes with your neighbor."

"I will. Talk to you soon. Love you." Summer disconnected, wanting to do something for Riley, but she could only do as much as Riley would allow.

With another glance at the clock, Summer gathered the necessary items and set the oven to preheat. As she prepared the dessert, she prayed for her sister and counted her blessings. If cooking a cobbler was the worst of Summer's worries, then she was in good shape. She had a terrific career as an occupational therapist in the elementary school system, she loved her apartment and its idealistic location, and she had tons of free time since school had let out for summer break.

Riley had been telling her for years she needed to get a social life. But if she was content to spend her evenings dog-sitting Chihuahuas, watching movies, and fretting over meeting her neighbor, who should tell her otherwise?

Summer chewed on her lower lip as the truth seeped through. She wouldn't mind dating someone. She wouldn't mind having someone to share laughs with or a shoulder to cry on when life's bumps came along.

Aiden Hawk had a shoulder. A nice, wide one.

She grinned as she mixed ingredients. Hopefully, she'd get a chance to speak to him within the hour.

After melting butter in the pan, she added the batter and sprinkled on blackberries. She slid the pan into the oven. Soon, she'd be ready to knock on his door.

But what if he had company?

Her nerves hummed.

Or what if he refused to answer? He *had* avoided her since his arrival.

She set the oven's timer.

Or maybe there was something innately wrong with him. He could have some kind of genetic mutation.

"Oh, good grief." Summer swiped stray sugar granules into her palm and dumped them into the trash. "He probably just doesn't want to meet you." Spoken aloud, that seemed the most likely scenario. Summer sighed at her own musings as she rinsed the mixing bowl.

A light knock sounded at her front door. She'd almost forgotten about Dottie's visit. Summer dried her hands, unlocked the door, and swung it wide.

Patches sat perched in Dottie's arms, tail wagging.

"Hey there, sweetheart." Summer patted his head.

He squirmed for freedom.

"Patience, Patches." Dottie's thick perfume followed her as she swept inside.

Summer shut the door and took a step back, preferring to avoid the perfume's strong scent, rather than mention the flowery fragrance made her eyes water, her throat close up, and her ears itch.

Dottie allowed Patches down.

He hit the floor running. Toenails clicked on the hardwood floor as he scrambled for the toy box.

Summer wasn't surprised when he sniffed the wicker basket and snatched up the new knotted rope she'd bought. "He knows where to look."

"You've spoiled him." Dottie clucked her tongue. "It's a wonder I get him to mind at all after he's spent time with you."

"Yes, I spoil him. But that's why you ask me to look after him, isn't it?"

Dottie's cherry-red lips turned up into a smile.

"Maybe." No maybes about it. Dottie adored her little companion.

And so did Summer. "You ready for your night out on the town? You look all fancied up."

"The outfit is new. Do you like it?" The pale blue slacks and matching patterned blouse fluttered as Dottie twirled in a circle, arms held wide.

The show made Dottie's perfume circulate, and Summer's allergies objected. "It looks nice on you." A sneeze threatened, and she eased toward the French doors.

"I told Frank I'd let him drive but it's not a date."

"Why not? He's a nice guy and he's about your age." Summer unlocked the doors and opened them. The fresh evening breeze blew in, and the need to sneeze abated, but her eyes still watered.

"He's fun to be around and all, but..." Dottie winked. "A girl's got to keep her options open."

Summer laughed. "So very true. Hope you have a good time."

"Oh, we will. With any luck I'll win the jackpot."

"What does the jackpot consist of this week?" From Dottie's previous explanations, Summer understood the fire station held bingo sessions to raise money for equipment and supplies, so instead of giving cash prizes, the department's volunteer firefighters and their families prepared homemade items like gift baskets, cakes, and jellies and jams for the winners. "Think they'll give away a batch of homemade ice cream again?"

"Oh, this time it's even better than rocky road or even pumpkin butter." Dottie paused to wiggle her gray brows. "It's a ticket to the fire department's twenty-first annual bachelor auction."

"They auction their men?" She'd heard of such things, but really? In the rural countryside, were there enough single women looking for dates? OK. So she was single, but still...

"Well, the Glade Springs station only has one contender, so all the fire departments in the region pool their resources, which results in a fabulous assortment."

"You sound as if you're talking about boxed chocolates."

"A group of physically fit, eligible bachelors is the next best thing, right?" Dottie pumped her eyebrows.

"And if you win?" Summer could only imagine the older woman going out with a young firefighter.

"If I win, I'll give you the ticket."

Summer blinked. "What? You're kidding, right?" Of course, Dottie couldn't know about her self-imposed rule. She'd yet to tell anyone she wouldn't date a man in a risky occupation. "I can get a date without paying for one."

Dottie waved away her comment. "It's for a good cause."

"There are lots of good causes needing support."

"Yes, but how many come with hunky dates?"

"I..." she began, but how could she argue with Dottie's reasoning? They were talking about one date, not a relationship. What were the odds Dottie would win the jackpot anyway? "I'll tell you what. If you win the ticket, I'll go to the auction and bid on the hottest guy there."

Dottie beamed and clapped hands. "I knew you had some fire in you."

Suspicion surfaced. "You're too happy. What do you know that you're not telling me?"

"Oh, look at the time." Checking her watch, Dottie stood and headed for the door. "I don't want to be late."

"Uh-huh." Summer pulled her lower lip between her teeth. Instinct told her she'd just been baited, hooked, and caught, all in one fell swoop.

Dottie paused at the door. "Don't forget to feed Patches at seven o'clock. He likes his dinner on time. Also, remember Frank lets his cat roam outdoors in the evenings. Whatever you do, do not let Tom near Patches. Patches will positively have a conniption."

"I'll keep that in mind."

"Good. I think that Tom cat enjoys teasing Patches." Dottie swept out the door.

Summer caught a whiff of perfume again and sneezed. "Patches, your momma is quite a character." She opened the French doors wider, sucking in fresh air.

Patches jumped onto Summer's couch, bringing the rope toy with him. He eyed her and mock growled, as if daring her to go after his new prized possession.

She pretended to lunge for the toy, and he defended his rope with a vicious snarl. "You can't fool me. Your wagging tail gives you away every time." She rubbed his fluffy fur.

Patches abandoned the toy and rolled onto his back for a belly rub.

Summer obliged. "You are adorable. But you know that already, don't you?"

When the oven's timer sounded, Summer checked the cobbler. The sweet scents surrounded her, overpowering the last of Dottie's lingering perfume. The edges had browned into a deep rich color and blackberries simmered throughout. A sense of accomplishment soared through her. Now, for the next step. She turned off the oven, grabbed mitts, and withdrew the pan. "Aiden Hawk. Ready or not, here I come." As nerves took hold, her finger slipped and touched the scalding pan. Jerking back, she set down the cobbler. She turned on the faucet and ran cold water over the searing pain. How much worse would a burn from a fire feel? She prayed she'd never know.

Patched whined, looking up from the couch.

"I'm all right..." Summer's voice failed as she caught a glimpse of a gray and white cat sauntering through the open doors. How had Tom managed to get onto her second-story balcony? "Oh no. Patches, don't look."

He looked.

A barrage of deep barks erupted, and it sounded as if Patches had grown into a full-sized bulldog and switched to attack mode. He scrambled from the couch and hit the floor running.

Tom cat hunched up his back, fur standing high, and danced in a circle around Patches.

Summer abandoned the water running in the sink and half ran, half slid her way across the kitchen and into the living room, her finger screaming with each step she took. "Patches, no."

Patches lunged.

Tom hissed and then, as if defying gravity, jumped straight up, paws spread wide. A curved claw caught on a lampshade, bringing Summer's favorite Tiffany lamp down on the cat. Tom screeched. Glass shattered, skittering across the floor.

Patches yelped and backed away to assess the situation, which gave Tom an opportunity to scale the couch, climb the canvas painting on the wall, and lunge toward the bookshelf where he managed to claw his way to safety on the top shelf.

Heart thundering, index finger throbbing, Summer pieced together all that had happened in the past couple of seconds. Tom was teasing the dog; he looked down from his perch with a triumphant smirk.

Patches barked so fast and hard his little back legs kept bouncing off the floor.

Summer wasn't about to touch either animal. She'd get mauled. She considered her options. At least the cobbler was out of the oven. She didn't have to worry about it burning, but the sweet scents reminded her she'd spent half the day gathering blackberries and baking a cobbler to break the ice with Aiden Hawk. This little incident was not about to ruin her plans. Lifting her chin, Summer clapped her hands. "Patches. Tom. Enough."

Patches didn't even break stride. His barks continued, some turning into high-pitched, frustrated yelps.

Tom cat looked at her, twitched an ear and then licked his paws.

They were at an impasse. Neither animal was about to give.

Maybe she should let them duke it out. It would serve them both right. But what would Dottie think if Patches got scratched or bitten? Summer would be banned from dog-sitting. And, if she couldn't handle that task, how would she eventually conquer motherhood?

"That's it. I've had enough." Summer marched around the kitchen bar, shut off the running water in the sink, and snatched the broom from the utility closet. As she approached Tom, his eyes widened.

"You asked for this." She nudged his backside with the bristles.

Tom dove for the doorway. The momentum knocked the tall bookshelf back, and it smacked against the wall. The painting hanging over the sofa lost its grip and clattered to the floor. Tom scrambled outside, leapt over the balcony's railing, and disappeared.

Pounding fists sounded on Summer's front door. "You OK in there?" a deep male voice boomed.

Patches yelped and ran for cover between Summer's feet. Caught off-guard, she stumbled and fell, landing on her rear with a jaw-shattering smack. The broom flew across the floor and knocked over a barstool. The loud crash pierced her ears.

"What's going on?" A fist pounded again. Louder. Faster.

Patches freaked and climbed up Summer as if she were a lifeboat on a sinking ship. His claws dug into her skin, leaving long white streaks that would soon turn into angry red welts.

"Stop, you're hurting me," she pleaded with Patches, but in his current panicked state, he continued to climb.

"I'm coming in." The man outside her door announced.

The front door slammed open with a loud, splintering crack. Shards of wood flew across the room, skidding across the hardwood floor as Aiden Hawk barged inside.

Patches dive-bombed the sofa, somehow squeezing his round little body underneath.

Mr. Hawk's assessing gaze took in Summer's prone form, and then he scanned the room. "What happened?" He strode across the floor, checked the balcony. "Did someone break in?"

Summer could only gape. Other than what looked to be steel-toe boots on his feet, he wore a pair of faded jeans and nothing else. Even half-dressed and armed with only two clenched fists, he looked more than ready and able to protect her.

But why would he? They hadn't even met yet. Not officially.

"Are you OK? Are you hurt?" He took a step forward as he looked her over. His gaze stopped at her bare arms.

She checked the damage. Dog claws had torn her up. The redness was beginning to show through. She rubbed her skin, thinking she was supposed to do something...oh yes.

Aiden Hawk had asked a question.

How could she respond? It looked as if her living room had been ransacked by intruders. Her backside ached, her burnt finger throbbed, and she had her neighbor's dog hiding under her couch. But yeah, she was OK. Relatively speaking.

"It was Tom." Summer shrugged without guilt. Let the cat take the blame.

"Is he still here?" Aiden looked past her. A muscle in his jaw ticked.

The slight movement distracted her. Not to mention the bare, tanned chest comprised of sculpted muscles. The man was simply gorgeous. And he was standing in her living room, filling the space with more testosterone than she'd experienced in...well, ever.

What was it he'd asked? Oh, yes. Tom. "He's gone. I went after him with a broom. He jumped off the balcony."

"A broom?" Confusion marred his brow. "He jumped off the balcony?"

"Yes."

"Wait." Aiden held up his hands. "You're telling me the guy who did this…"

Summer didn't hear the rest of his words. *The guy who did this*? Realization dawned. She had made an assumption that Aiden had met Tom. She could only imagine what he was thinking. "Tom is Frank's cat."

Aiden's brows lifted. "Ah, that makes more sense."

"I left the doors open. Tom wandered inside. Patches had a fit. One thing led to another. My lamp broke. My picture fell. You thought I was in trouble, and…" She glanced toward the front door swinging wide. The wood frame had splintered. But that was OK. She had Aiden Hawk talking and that was worth any repair bill.

His gaze followed hers. "I heard things crashing, and when you didn't answer, I thought someone was hurting you." He tucked his hands into his pockets as a slight blush rose up his cheeks. "Sorry about the door."

He'd done what not many others would've attempted. "No apology needed." She climbed to her feet and took a few steps toward him. "I'm Summer Cassel."

"Aiden Hawk." He shook her outstretched hand and then returned his calloused palm to his pocket. He looked around everywhere but at her. He picked up the painting and set it back on the wall, taking care to make it level.

"Thanks."

"No problem."

An awkward silence ensued. Where did her

fearless rescuer go? Perhaps he managed crisis situations better than ordinary life. She wanted to ask but didn't want to embarrass him.

Summer grabbed the broom and began sweeping the lamp's shattered pieces. "Patches, it's OK. You don't have to hide anymore."

A little nose sniffed the air from beneath the couch, but no dog emerged.

Aiden stepped toward the door. "I should go—"

"No. Wait." Summer stopped sweeping.

Aiden stopped walking.

She stared into his expectant eyes. It seemed strange that he would look directly at her when he thought she needed something. Otherwise, he appeared almost...shy. She sucked in a breath. Of course. That was it. He didn't think she had a disease. He was being bashful. How cute.

She looked around for something to keep him engaged in conversation. No telling how long before she would have an opportunity to speak with him again, and apparently, they'd yet to actually break any ice. Now would be an unlikely time to offer the man blackberry cobbler, though, with all that had happened and the mess she had to clean up. And how would she get Patches to come out before Dottie returned?

Still, she had to say something. Maybe she could get him to come back later. "Do you have plans tonight?"

Aiden straightened and cleared his throat. "I was on my way to bed when I heard the crash."

So much for sharing dessert with him. "Oh." Now that he mentioned it, he did look rather fatigued. His hair was rumpled and he had faint dark circles under his eyes. "Sorry to keep you up."

"It's OK. I could've ignored the sounds."

"Yes. But you didn't." She flashed an appreciative smile.

He ducked his head, turned, and inspected the broken doorframe. Probably so he wouldn't have to make eye contact again. "Looks like I just splintered the wood. Should be a fairly easy fix. I'll check the shed and see if Frank's got some tools I can use. I'll be back in a few." He turned and fled the apartment as if she had become the threat.

"Well, that went well." Summer turned to Patches. "You can come out now. Or are you afraid of me too?"

3

Aiden stopped by his apartment and grabbed a T-shirt, and then took the steps two at a time. He needed air. Lots of it. His palms wouldn't stop sweating. Even his forehead had begun to perspire. Had Summer noticed? Did it matter? He'd already made a fool of himself busting into her apartment like a one-man SWAT team. Although she hadn't appeared upset and had even introduced herself, she certainly would think his actions overkill.

It's not as if she had been screaming for his intervention. But she had been gracious about the whole thing. She'd even asked if he'd had plans tonight.

He'd made it sound as if he'd rather sleep than spend any more time with her, which was *so* not the case. He should've explained he'd been up most of the previous night responding to emergency calls, but he'd been too nervous to utter the words. At this rate, he'd be single for the rest of his life. Then again, it wasn't all women he was tongue-tied around, just Summer.

He sighed, drove fingers though his hair, and deliberately slowed his steps. Frank kept maintenance tools and equipment inside the larger of the two sheds out back. He'd take a peek and see if there was something he could use inside. If not, he'd have to run into Glade Springs to the hardware store, a twenty-minute drive each way. But that would take too long. In spite of his nerves, he wanted to get back to

Summer, and not only to repair the door, but also to salvage his dignity before catching up on some sleep. If he could sleep after this.

Lord, let there be something in the shed I can use.

Aiden stepped outside. The view from the apartment complex never ceased to amaze him. Rolling hills led to waves of mountains in the distance, while the river's constant flow soothed. He'd picked this place to call home the moment he'd seen the pictures in the real estate magazine. With his thirst for adventure, having the Shenandoah River at his backdoor had proven to be an asset.

He strode across the lawn and swung the shed's doors open wide, thankful Frank didn't need to keep the shed locked. Crime wasn't exactly rampant around Glade Springs, which was something he should've remembered before breaking into Summer's apartment.

Aiden shook his head. Nothing he could do about that now but repair the damage. He stepped inside the shed, disturbing dust particles and spider webs. To the left, ropes, cables, and various lawn equipment occupied the space. To the right, Frank's workshop bench sat covered with hammers, handsaws, screwdrivers, and ratchets. A pegboard on the wall held all sorts of gadgets, but nothing he could use to fix a doorframe.

Aiden checked the drawers beneath the bench and found a putty knife, a clamp, and wood glue waiting, as if Frank had experienced a break-in before. Aiden was fairly confident no one but him had kicked through Summer's door to rescue her from Tom, the cat.

Given different circumstances, he could laugh

about it. Maybe one day he would sit on the porch with Summer and reminisce about it over fresh-squeezed lemonade.

Aiden's imagination had run away with him more than once. He'd told himself to stop fantasizing. He'd be lucky if Summer Cassel ever wanted to talk to him again. He gathered the necessary items, picked up some old rags just in case, and shut the door.

Summer was waiting for him when he returned to her apartment. The enticing, sweet aroma of whatever it was she'd cooked still lingered in the air, making the place feel welcoming. Or maybe it was Summer's smile that drew him in.

She stood beside a coffee table with Patches in her arms, petting him as if not sure what else to do. She had cleaned up the broken lamp and had placed the splintered wood pieces on a table beside the door within easy reach. She was efficient and thoughtful.

He liked that—he liked a lot of things about her.

Aiden set down the tools but remained in the doorway. He paused, steeled his nerves. He didn't want to appear rude and not speak to her. He could do this. He'd been talking since he was one-and-a-half years old. He searched for a neutral topic. "Patches and I usually get along fine. Sorry I spooked him."

"It's all right. He's OK now." She scratched Patches behind his ears. "He was already rattled by Tom cat by the time you broke through the door."

Aiden cringed at the reminder. But at least they'd finally met each other. He knelt and went to work, concentrating on the task before him. Well, as much as he could concentrate with Summer observing. A heightened sense of awareness kept him alert to each of her subtle movements. The longer he worked, the greater the intensity; the greater the intensity, the more jangled his nerves became.

Several times she tried to make small talk.

Several times he attempted an adequate response, but he managed only a few one or two syllable words. By the time he finished the door, the urge to escape overwhelmed. Aiden's heart pounded so fast he feared she'd see the evidence pulsating at his neck. And his palms had dampened to the point where giving her a parting handshake was out of the question.

He collected the supplies. "Let the clamp stay on the door until the glue dries. Then you'll be all set." Aiden left Summer staring after him, no doubt wondering what kind of lunatic had moved in next door.

4

As darkness fell, Summer closed her curtains, resigned to the fact that Aiden had fled her apartment as if he couldn't get away fast enough. Considering her past experiences with him, she shouldn't be surprised.

Summer sighed and inspected the repaired doorframe. No visible cracks remained, and she was certain the door would look as good as new once she removed the clamp. But it was too soon for that. She'd have to allow the door to sit open for now; the glue still looked shiny and wet.

Unsure what to do in the meantime, she eyed the door a little while longer. She'd heard of the term watching grass grow, but watching glue dry? That was a new concept. Yeah, she needed to get a life.

Summer allowed her thoughts to change directions. She straightened the books lining her bookshelf. Every one of them had been knocked out of place when Tom had banged the shelf against the wall. When she finished with the books, she set about fluffing throw pillows, and then used a wide strip of tape to remove dog hairs from her sofa's upholstery.

Patches watched as she flitted about the living room, his little eyeballs swiveling with each pass she made around the coffee table.

But no matter what small task she accomplished, her thoughts always returned to Aiden. He was good at fixing things. That was a bonus, in case she needed help in the future. Not that she'd go knocking on his door if her kitchen faucet sprang a leak. He obviously didn't want to hang out too long. So why did she look forward to their next encounter? "What do you think, Patches?" She stood in front of the dog. "Am I wasting my time trying to be nice to this guy?"

If only dogs could talk. Patches would have some wise recommendations. He was a smart animal, she could tell. As she looked into his eyes, it appeared he understood her dilemma. He tilted his head and whimpered.

"Yeah. I don't think so either." Any man who would go out of his way to protect someone he didn't even know, deserved to be given the benefit of the doubt.

For now, she needed to concentrate on getting her life in order, or to be more exact, getting her social life on track. Ever since she'd moved to Shenandoah Valley, her focus had been on settling into her career and in acclimating herself to the rural environment. Now that she had those things under control, it was time to review what was missing in her life. A familiar sense of loneliness crept in.

She glanced at Patches. She could get a dog.

A soft knock sounded, bringing Summer from her thoughts.

Dottie appeared in the doorway. Patches perked up his ears and scrambled from the couch. He launched into her arms and set about licking her face. Now, that was devotion.

But not exactly the brand of affection Summer yearned for.

"Oh, my." Dottie allowed Patches to swoon over her. "I missed you, too." She looked at the clamped doorframe. "What happened?"

"It's kind of a long story." Summer relaxed onto the couch and invited Dottie to sit. "Let's talk about your evening first. Did you have a good time?"

Dottie had an extra brightness in her eyes and a bounce in her step as she crossed the room and sank onto Summer's recliner. "I did. It's always nice to get out. And Frank treats me like a lady." She fanned her face. "I tell you, there's a shortage of gentlemen these days. Aren't we blessed? We have two of them living in the same building with us."

"Yes, we are."

"This way," —Dottie settled Patches in her lap— "when Frank's gone off on his cruise these next few weeks, we won't be alone. Aiden will be around."

Summer had been fending for herself for so long, she'd learned to appreciate a helping hand now and then, but it wasn't as if she'd had any trouble since moving to The Meadows. Well, except from Tom cat. Summer pulled a throw pillow onto her lap. "Any news on who is going to rent the last vacant apartment?"

"Funny you mention that. We talked about it tonight. Frank's denied all but one of the applicants. A pediatrician, works out of Luray. Frank is concerned the long commute would get tiresome, but the young doctor assures Frank that he enjoys driving in the countryside and that The Meadows is exactly what he's looking for."

"I understand that. I fell in love with this place the first time I saw it."

"I think all of us did." Dottie rubbed Patches a little faster than normal. "But that's not all the news I have for you tonight."

"What is it?"

"I hope you remember your promise."

"My promise?" So much had happened since Dottie had left that Summer struggled to recall.

Dottie whipped out a rectangular piece of paper from her purse. "That if I won a ticket, you would attend the Glade Springs Volunteer Fire Department's bachelor auction and bid on the hottest guy there."

"No way." She accepted the paper as Dottie handed it over. It had the fire department's emblem embossed across the top and a VIP invitation clearly scripted on the bottom. "You won?"

Dottie nodded so enthusiastically her hair bobbed along with her chin. "Front row ticket."

Summer's fluttering stomach twisted into a knot. "What if I changed my mind? I can still donate money."

"Oh, no you don't. You're not squirming out of this. You promised."

She had. But still... "That's when I thought you had little chance of winning."

Dottie waved a hand and chuckled. "Of course I had a good chance. There were only five other people there, and I bought three times as many bingo cards as anyone else in the room."

"Five other people? Including Frank?"

"Yep."

"But I thought there were usually at least thirty or forty players?"

"There are, normally. But with the other activities going on tonight—the annual fish fry at Brookside Baptist Church, the free coffee special at Tyler's Donuts, and the premiere of that new action film—the others were busy elsewhere."

"You sneak," Summer chastised. "You knew you

had an excellent chance of winning."

"Well, of course, dear." Dottie petted Patches. "You didn't think I'd leave such a thing to chance, did you?" She leaned in. "And, from what I've seen, your love life could use a little boost."

Summer scoffed. "Just because I dog-sit on Friday nights doesn't mean—"

Dottie's brows lifted, but she didn't say anything, because she didn't need to.

"OK. Fine. So I don't get out much." She stopped short of telling Dottie she was happy with her present circumstances, because in truth, she wasn't entirely satisfied.

"This is your chance to get into the fray."

Maybe attending a bachelor auction and securing a one-time, no-strings-attached date was what she needed. Besides, it was for a good cause. "I guess I could go and at least see what it's like."

"And…bid on the hottest guy there."

"Right. Thanks for the reminder." She shifted. "So, how many men will be part of the auction?"

"I'm guessing around a dozen or so."

"Do you know anything about them?" With Dottie spending so much time at the station, surely she would know something.

Dottie grinned. "I know the one stationed at Glade Springs."

"What's he like?"

"Why so serious? This is supposed to be fun."

Something about the way Dottie evaded Summer's question made her suspicious. "What are you up to?"

Dottie absently patted Patches as her gaze strayed across the room. "Something looks different. Wasn't there a lamp in that corner before?"

"Yeah. There was until a little while ago."

"And you haven't told me about the door yet. What happened?"

"Tom happened." Summer went on to explain the evening's fiasco, detailing each of the events. By the time she'd finished, Dottie was clutching her sides as laughter wracked her body. Summer had to admit what happened sounded rather comical.

"I declare, you need a keeper." Dottie giggled and stood and made her way to the door. "I guess we'd better get going. Thanks again for watching Patches." She scooted out without answering Summer's question.

Dottie was up to something, but what could it be?

5

Summer wouldn't be uncovering what Dottie was planning tonight, but she would sooner or later. She only hoped whatever it was turned out to be a good thing. For now, she checked the door again. She tapped at the glue, and it felt dry, so she removed the clamp. As she'd suspected, the frame looked almost brand new. Who knew her neighbor was so talented?

She should thank him. She glanced at the cobbler again and then at her blistered finger and scratched arms. Her first homemade blackberry cobbler might very well be her last, and she really shouldn't let it go to waste. She should take it to Aiden. After all, the way to a man's heart was through his stomach. But then again, she wasn't after his heart.

Liar. Her conscience called her out.

Fine. So she was interested in Aiden Hawk. Too bad he made a habit of avoiding her. Maybe he already had a girlfriend. Or an ex he still loved. Just because he appeared to be a handsome, eligible bachelor didn't mean he was one. Not the handsome part, of course. He was good-looking. That was obvious. But the eligible part, she really had no way of knowing other than outright asking.

She'd rather go back to the blackberry brambles during midday heat than ask Aiden if he was emotionally attached to someone. She'd be moved to the top of his crazy-cat-lady-neighbor list. Except she didn't have a cat.

Maybe she should get one.

Summer expelled a frustrated breath. When had life become so complicated? She had spent way too much time thinking about her neighbor in the past few weeks. It was time to get her mind on something else. But in order to move on, she needed to finish with the whole cobbler thing.

She spun her ruby ring around her finger; the gift her sister had given her when she'd obtained her master's degree had been a source of comfort in stressful situations. Should she dare go over there and knock? Aiden had said he needed to catch up on his sleep. What if she woke him? Well, she could always step to his door and listen. If she heard noises inside his apartment, she'd know he was awake.

Decision made, Summer picked up the cobbler. She exited her apartment and walked the ten steps across the hall to Aiden's door. The old hotel's original crystal chandelier hung overhead, casting the paneled wood in a soft, welcoming glow. As if the historic building lived and breathed, a breeze drifted up the open staircase and circulated around the space, cooling her warm skin. She welcomed the sensation, calming the nerves that had begun to hum.

Summer knew what lay beyond the door. She'd explored apartment 2B before Aiden had moved in. The layout was much the same as hers, the view was too, but the kitchen had a little less counter space, and it had one-and-a-half bathrooms instead of two.

The apartment would look different occupied. She visualized Aiden in the space. Was he the bachelor-pad type? Bare bones and functional? Or did he add more detail to his surroundings and cozy up the place?

Only one way to find out. She adjusted the cobbler in her hand, leaned in, and pressed an ear to the door. A noise sounded from within. He must be up and moving around.

Encouraged, Summer fisted her hand, brought her knuckles close to the door...and then lost her nerve. What if she was wrong? She'd wake him, and her good gesture would backfire. She reviewed her options. She'd either have to go through with this or—

The door swung open, Summer lost her balance and tumbled inside. She plowed into Aiden Hawk's hard chest—and so did the cobbler. The dessert oozed in chunks down his T-shirt, rolled off his jeans, and plopped to the hardwood floor.

Summer froze and then looked up into Aiden's wide, sapphire eyes. "Um...w-welcome to The Meadows?"

~*~

Taken off-guard, Aiden took a reflexive step back. Something gooey squished beneath his boot.

Summer appeared to have stopped breathing. Her eyes glimmered as if tears fought for release. "I...uh...made a blackberry cobbler for you to welcome you to the building. I was just about to knock when—" She glanced over the dessert smattered on his clothes. "I'm so sorry."

Although sticky warmth penetrated his shirt and dark stains splotched his jeans, he didn't lose momentum. As much as he'd like to reassure her everything was OK, he simply didn't have the time. "I have to go." He'd make it up to her later. Somehow. He stepped past her and ran toward the stairs, certain he was tracking dessert across the floor. He spared a glance at Summer. The astonished look on her pale face would haunt him, but what choice did he have? "Lock the door for me, will you?"

Not waiting for a reply, he took the steps two at a time, jogged to his truck, and climbed inside. At least the seats were leather and easily cleanable. As for his ruined T-shirt and jeans, he had plenty to spare. He cranked the engine and jammed the vehicle into gear.

Adrenaline had been buzzing through his veins since Captain Warren had called and asked him to pitch in to help extinguish a brush fire. Although the forecast called for rain in the upcoming week, the recent drought and high winds made for dangerous conditions. Especially since the fire was burning just northeast of Glade Springs's historic district.

Aiden pressed the accelerator as he drove along the tree-lined road leading away from The Meadows. Darkness had set in, casting shadows across the land. He flipped his headlights to high beam and gripped the wheel as the urgency to reach his destination spurred him forward.

After fifteen minutes, the burning field came into view. Several acres had been charred, the vegetation reduced to ashes. Firefighters had maneuvered the brush truck close to the blaze and Engine 11 served as backup. Aiden recognized several personal vehicles. Apparently, he hadn't been the only off-duty personnel called.

He parked on the road's shoulder, exited his truck. The thick scent of burning brush blanketed the normally fresh country air, bringing with it a heightened sense of apprehension. If the flames travelled another mile south, commercial buildings would burn.

Aiden maneuvered his way past various apparatuses, stepped over a fire hose, and scanned the area. He caught a glimpse of a red helmet and headed for Captain Warren.

Worry lines creased the captain's weary features. Dark blond hair streaked with silver stuck out from beneath his helmet, his gray eyes intent. "Glad you made it," he yelled over the surrounding chaos. "Grab your turnout gear and..." His gaze landed on Aiden's T-shirt and his eyes widened. "Are you hurt?"

Aiden glanced down. Now dry, the blackberry stains could be mistaken as blood smears in the dim light. "I'm fine." He raised his voice above the sounds of the crackling flames, idling engines, and streaming water hoses. "It's not what it looks like. I ran into my neighbor on the way over here."

"The woman you've been telling me about?"

Aiden nodded. "I'm wearing my housewarming gift."

Captain Warren lifted a brow. "That's a first."

"What can I say? It's been an eventful day."

"You'll have to tell me about it sometime. For now, get suited up and head over to the southeastern perimeter with Marilyn and William. I need you to help them with the firebreak." He turned away, and then as if on second thought, glanced back and scanned Aiden's marred shirt again. "That neighbor of yours must be something else."

If he only knew. "She's unforgettable." Aiden jogged toward the fire engine and found his turnout gear ready and waiting. Once fully dressed, he picked up a Pulaski and headed out, gripping the ax-and-hoe combination tool tight as he prepared for the grueling night ahead.

6

It had been a couple of days since Summer had smeared cobbler all over Aiden, and she'd yet to see him again. She'd obliterated every speck of dust from her apartment, washed and ironed the curtains, vacuumed under the couch, and rearranged her file cabinet all while hoping Aiden would show up so she could make amends.

She'd looked for his truck so often, she resembled a stalker. Enough was enough. She'd eventually have the opportunity to apologize and then it would be over. He had his life. She had hers. Considering their unusual encounters, it was probably better this way.

Summer rearranged everything on her coffee table, and with nothing left to do, boredom struck. She could fill her spare time volunteering as a hiking guide at Shenandoah National Park—except she didn't like bears, and people ran into them in the Blue Ridge Mountains every day. Her mind spun with other possibilities. She could apply for a guide position at Luray Caverns and lead visitors through the earth's deep, dark recesses—except she had claustrophobic tendencies.

Sighing, Summer paced the apartment. She didn't remember being this antsy any summer before this, and she'd been working within various school systems for the past seven years. Of course, before this year she'd lived close to Riley and had hung out with her. But as much as Summer missed her sister, she'd felt called to Shenandoah Valley.

Lord, I believe You want me here for a reason. This is my home now, but I miss Riley and Zack so much. Please reveal to me why I'm here. What is it that You want me to do?

The digital clock on her cable TV box counted the minutes as she sank onto the couch and waited for an answer. She often prayed and then listened. Sometimes answers came from reading her Bible. Sometimes they came in a knowing deep in her heart. Other times, answers evaded her altogether. This time, her own thoughts distracted her as they kept drifting back to Aiden.

Exasperated, Summer opened the French doors and stepped onto the balcony. A hundred yards away, the Shenandoah River meandered past, inviting her to enjoy all it had to offer. Without a second thought, she accepted that invitation. She hurried into her apartment, changed into a tank top and khaki shorts, and then planted a baseball cap on her head. After applying a coat of sun block and gathering a few snacks and a water bottle, she loaded her backpack, grabbed her keys and cellphone, and headed outside. The afternoon temperatures soared into the upper nineties, but clouds rolled past, giving relief from the midday heat.

She tried not to notice Aiden's vacant parking spot. But she did. He hadn't been home in days. Where did the man go for so long?

"Not my business," Summer reminded herself as she trotted past the graveled lot, over the manicured lawn, and to the shed that housed the kayaks. When Frank returned home, she'd have to thank him for the unlimited use of the river equipment.

Four kayaks rested on racks inside the shed. Only two were made for one person: the canary-yellow kayak that she'd used last time, and the royal blue one, which happened to be the larger of the two. She hadn't tried that one yet. She shrugged. Might as well go for something different. She eased the boat from the rack, but it was heavier than she'd imagined, and it thudded to the ground, narrowly missing her toes. Unable to lift the boat, she dragged it to the shoreline. The exertion brought out a layer of perspiration, but she didn't mind. She expected to get hot on this trip.

After selecting a paddle and zipping into a life preserver, Summer shoved the boat into the water, climbed in, and settled her backpack within easy reach. She soon cleared the rocky shore and entered the river's main channel.

A light breeze carried scents of the river's fresh water, and nature's quiet stillness surrounded her. The river offered freedom as if the pressures of the world couldn't breach the shoreline. Peace descended and a sense of calm reigned.

Thank You, Lord, for leading me to Shenandoah.

She fell into a rhythm as she stroked the paddle through the water. As she neared the first bend, her cellphone chimed. Setting the paddle across her lap, Summer searched the backpack. She hadn't paid attention to which pocket she'd placed the phone. She checked the outer flap. Not there. The main compartment. Nope. She turned the backpack and found it in the side pocket.

Riley's number appeared on the caller ID.

Summer answered. "Hey. I thought I was going to miss your call."

The river's current caught the kayak, reversing the

boat's momentum, and she began floating downriver.

"I don't know what I'm going to do with Zack." Riley's shaky voice caught Summer's full attention, and she allowed the boat to drift.

"What do you mean? What's happened?" Her nerves stretched tight.

"He's been caught shoplifting again. Leonard managed to keep him out of jail, but he said he can't keep protecting Zack."

Summer remembered Leonard was Doug's partner. He had taken it upon himself to look after Riley and Zack since Doug's passing. He'd proven to have a generous spirit, but apparently, his patience had worn thin.

"The Zack I knew would never have stolen anything. What's happened to him?" Summer asked, but she already knew the answer. Losing his father had sent her nephew's behavior into a downward spiral.

Riley's pause lasted so long, Summer thought she might've lost the connection. "He's become a teenager, and he is hanging out with the wrong crowd. Last night I caught him wearing gang colors."

Numbing fear gripped Summer, and she clenched the cellphone tight. The kayak picked up speed, succumbing to the river's pull. She drifted past The Meadows, heading in a direction she hadn't explored before. She'd never allowed herself to float downriver for fear of not making it back, but the possibility barely registered as she concentrated on her sister.

"His behavior has been getting worse since school let out. He's got too much time to spend with those...juvenile delinquents. I have to work. I can't be home all day to make sure he's not getting into trouble." Riley's voice cracked.

"I shouldn't have left you." Guilt tugged at Summer.

"Oh, stop. This isn't about you." Riley snapped and then paused, softening her voice. "I'm sorry. I...I just don't know what I'm going to do."

"No need to apologize." Summer could only imagine the pressure Riley faced. Judging by her last response, Summer offering to move back in wasn't the best choice. Another thought struck. "Zack can come here and live with me until school starts again."

Seconds ticked by. "He's all I have left."

"Glade Springs doesn't have gangs." Summer pointed out.

"I don't know. Let me think about it." Riley's voice continued to quiver. "I don't know what's best for him."

What was best for Zack might be getting away from his so-called friends for a while.

Summer's heart raced with the possibility of taking on full responsibility for her nephew, but it made sense. She had a spare bedroom and she had the time. Is this what God had in mind for her for the next few months?

Maybe, but even so, her chest squeezed tight. The level of responsibility sent chills over her arms, even in the warm climate. But she had offered, and if Riley needed her, she'd do everything in her power to help. "I'm here for you and Zack. Say the word and I'll come get him."

Riley let out a humorless chuckle. "As the older sister, I always thought I was supposed to look after you."

"You always have. Now, it's my turn."

"We'll see. I need to go. I'll call you soon." Riley

disconnected, leaving Summer's mind spinning.

Tucking her cellphone into the backpack, Summer looked around and her stomach sank. She didn't recognize any landmarks and had no idea how far the water had washed her downriver. She grabbed the paddle, turned the kayak, and stroked hard to propel herself against the current.

No signs of civilization appeared on either side of the river, and The Meadows was long gone. She had studied maps of the winding Shenandoah, but the hand-drawn sketches looked nothing like her real-world surroundings.

A rumble of thunder echoed across the valley, and a sense of unease stole her remaining peace. Dark clouds rolled in and cast the area in shadows. At least the drought would soon be over; lucky for the farmers, not so lucky for her. Was the river already flowing faster?

Summer's muscles protested as she dug the paddle into the water deeper and stroked harder, but the river continued to win the battle. With no choice but to concede, she allowed the current to take over.

No doubt remained—the water flow had increased. Perhaps the rain had already begun nearby, swelling the river. No wonder she hadn't seen anyone else out. They'd probably all watched the weather forecast.

She'd heard of the many rescues Glade Springs's first responders had carried out in the past when the water levels rose quickly, and she prayed she wouldn't need such resources. But as she fought to maintain her calm, the possibility kept creeping into her thoughts.

A sharp crack of thunder split the air, and Summer cringed.

Lord, help me get off this river before the storm arrives.

~*~

Aiden steered his truck along the winding road leading to The Meadows. After the night he'd spent dousing the brushfire, he'd slept at the station, only to awaken and fulfill another twenty-four-hour shift. At least now he'd have some free time until the bachelor auction rolled around.

He hadn't agreed to take part in the fundraiser yet, but pressure mounted. In recent months, two fire hoses had burst, a pump had gone down on Engine 12, and three volunteers needed replacement turnout gear. He wanted to do his part, but the thought of parading in front of women seeking men in uniforms didn't appeal in the slightest.

He'd rather concentrate on one woman—a woman who didn't fall for a man because of what he did for a living, but rather for his character. He didn't know if Summer Cassel was that type, but he wanted to find out. Over the past several days, he'd had ample time to think about her. He was still amazed she'd offered a housewarming gift after the way he'd barged in on her.

As he approached the apartment building, his nerves amped up. He wanted to clear the air, make certain she didn't feel bad about the other night. He only hoped he could push past his stubborn shy streak and have a normal conversation with her.

Aiden parked next to Summer's SUV. Thankful she was home, he strode into The Meadows with a clear purpose in mind. Taking the stairs two at a time, Aiden aimed for apartment 2A. He knocked before he lost his nerve. She didn't answer. He knocked again.

Dottie emerged from her apartment. "I thought I heard someone out here."

Patches scuttled under her feet and ran toward Aiden.

He scooped up the dog. "Glad to see you're not afraid of me anymore."

Patches answered with a lick to Aiden's chin.

Dottie grinned. "If you're looking for Summer, she went out in the kayak a couple hours ago. I don't think she's back yet."

Aiden's easy smile fell. "She's on the river? There's a storm heading this way. We're expecting several inches of rain." He returned Patches. "I'd better go check on her."

"Let me know if you find her." Dottie rubbed the dog's fur a little too fast.

"Will do." Aiden retraced his steps, shoved through the foyer doors, and crossed the parking lot. He checked the storage shed, counted three kayaks.

One was missing.

His muscles grew taut. He trained his gaze on the river, its current flowing swift and strong. The wind had picked up and thunder echoed across the mountains. He edged toward the shoreline, careful to avoid the slippery rocks. Looking both ways, he confirmed his fear.

Summer was nowhere in sight.

The air carried the scent of rain. If she didn't return soon...

"Aiden." Dottie appeared on the wraparound porch. She stood beside one of several rocking chairs, waving her arms.

He jogged toward her.

"Summer just called. The current carried her

downriver. She's managed to pull onto a narrow bank but she can't paddle back. The water's moving too fast."

At least she was OK. Aiden would've allowed relief to settle in, but she wasn't out of the woods yet. "She needs to find shelter before the storm hits."

"That's why she called. I told her I'd send help. You were the first person I thought of."

He nodded, considering the best course of action. If he went after her in a kayak, they'd both become stranded in the storm. He stepped toward his truck. "I'll go get her. Where is she?"

"That's the problem. She doesn't know."

7

Summer's initial relief didn't last long as common sense took over. Dottie had promised to send someone to pick her up, but what good would that do if she couldn't tell anyone where she had landed?

She double-checked the kayak's rope that she'd tied to a tree and sat on a bed of fallen leaves. As if nearby animals and insects had already taken shelter from the storm, the rushing river made the only sound. At least she was off the water. She'd be safe enough even if she had to flip the kayak and seek shelter underneath.

Thunder rumbled again, vibrating the earth beneath her.

Then again, maybe not.

She scooted away from a towering tree only to find herself butted up against another. In a forest, what could she expect? Well, at least she hadn't run across any bears. Yet.

Summer sighed. She had to stay focused. A little granola bar would help. She sifted through her backpack, digging out the food. She ripped open the package and took a bite before another disconcerting thought hit her. What if a bear caught the scent? Her gaze darted every which way. Was that a shadow moving behind that boulder?

Her cellphone rang. She jumped and her snack tumbled onto the dirt. This situation kept getting better and better. Heart pounding, she managed to answer the call.

"Summer. It's Aiden. I heard you could use a ride home." The deep, rich timbre of his voice connected her with humanity again, instantly grounding her.

"So you're not mad at me for dumping the blackberry cobbler all over you?"

"I was actually hoping you'd make another one for me sometime."

"Oh." The unexpected comment would've knocked her off her feet, had she been standing. "I'll think about it."

"Fair enough. For now, let's concentrate on getting you home."

"Easier said than done." She looked around. "I don't know where I am."

"I can help you with that." His tone held underlying confidence. "What time did you leave The Meadows?"

Why hadn't she noticed how attractive his voice was before? Oh yeah. She'd been too busy admiring his physical attributes. Besides, he'd barely spoken more than a few words to her, much less in complete sentences. Why the sudden change? Was it because they were talking on the phone and not face to face?

"Summer?"

"Yes. I'm here." She considered his question. "I'm not sure what time I left, but I paddled upstream for a few minutes before my sister called."

"Check your cellphone. See what time you received her call."

Good idea. "Hold on." She pressed buttons, and when she found the time, she returned the phone to her ear. "Riley called about an hour ago."

"How long have you been on shore?"

"Less than ten minutes."

"All right. That gives us something to work with."

"I like where you're headed with this." Her hopes rose. Maybe with Aiden's assistance she could avoid the storm after all. "What else can I tell you?"

"Do you remember seeing any identifiable landmarks?"

"No. It's all trees and fields around here." The possibility of bears nearby came to mind again, but the thought didn't scare her as much with Aiden on the line. "I haven't seen anyone else the entire time I've been on the water."

"I'm here and I'm not leaving you." His confident tone turned soothing. "Have you passed a cabin on the right?"

"Not that I noticed, but I could have."

"How many bends have you gone around?"

"I...don't know. A couple, maybe?"

Thunder rumbled again, growing ever closer.

Her nerves pitched a fit. "I'm not helping much, am I?"

"You're doing fine. I'm driving north on River Road, which parallels the river for quite a ways. We're probably already within a few miles of each other. Now it's a matter of pinpointing your exact location."

"I can start walking and see if I can find a road or someone's house."

"It's better if you remain where you are for now. The river gives us a point of reference. Have you run into any rapids?"

"Haven't noticed any."

"You would notice the ones I'm thinking about. They cover the entire width of the river."

Summer clung to his steady voice. "Are you

always this calm when you're rescuing someone?"

He let out a small chuckle. "I've got some experience to back me up."

"I'd like to hear about it sometime." Another gust of wind warned of the approaching storm. "But for now, I want out of here."

"Working on it. Have you seen a boat ramp and a dock on your right side?"

"No. I don't think so." She would've seen it, wouldn't she? "How do you know so much about the river?"

"I grew up in Shenandoah Valley, at Hope Haven Children's Home. I practically lived on the water."

"Hope Haven?" Summer had heard of the place. "Isn't that an—"

"Orphanage? Yes."

"Oh, I'm sorry." She never would've guessed he'd been raised without his natural parents.

"No need to be sorry. God has always made sure I have all I need."

Warmth infused her at the mention of his faith. "Me too. And right now, I need you. Thanks for doing this."

"Not a problem. I'm not the type to leave someone stranded."

"I noticed. I assumed since you were new to The Meadows—"

"That I was new to the area? Not at all. I did move away for a while to go to college and start my career. But I returned a few years ago."

The more she learned about Aiden, the more she wanted to know, but the scent of rain grew stronger and the river's current continued to increase speed. "The conditions are getting worse. I need to do something."

"Do you have a lifejacket?"

"Of course."

"Are you wearing it?"

"I was, but I took it off when I got to land."

"Put it on. You're going back in the water."

Summer's heart jolted. "I am?"

"I need you to float a ways downriver. I'll be waiting for you at the boat ramp we just talked about."

"How do you know I'm not past it already?"

"I don't. Not for certain."

"I appreciate your honesty." A fallen tree sailed past on the river at amazing speed. "But I don't like your idea. It's risky."

"Life's full of risks. Sometimes taking a chance is the only way to know if something will work."

"And if it doesn't?"

"Then we'll try something else."

Summer hesitated. "Not if I get struck by lightning first."

"I need you to trust me on this." His calm demeanor coupled with his direct and specific instructions made her pause.

"You sound so self-assured, it's hard to believe I'm talking to the same guy who blushes and turns away every time I try to talk to him."

Aiden hesitated, and then spoke in low tones. "Things aren't always as they seem."

Very true. She'd have to wait and see how he reacted to her in person again. The complexity of the man intrigued her. "I'll get in the boat, if you promise to stay on the line."

"I'll try, but there are sections of the river without cell service. We might lose each other."

From the moment she'd first heard his voice on the phone, he'd become her connection to civilization. The thought of losing that security caused anxiety to surface. She tugged on the lifejacket, zipping it tight with shaky fingers.

"I've seen you handle the kayak before. Summer, you are more than capable of doing this on your own."

She liked how he'd used her name and given her credit, which boosted her confidence. Almost seemed as if he'd been trained to do this sort of thing. She untied the rope, stepped into the kayak, and shoved from shore, all the while keeping the cellphone pressed tight to her ear. "I'm on the water."

"All right. I'll be waiting for you. If you can, stick to the left side of the river for now. There are less dangerous rapids on that side."

Her newfound confidence washed downstream as fast as the fallen tree. "Dangerous?"

"Keep paddling, you'll be fine. Set aside the phone if you need to."

She maneuvered around a group of rocks protruding from the water. "I'd rather hear your voice."

"I want to stay connected to you, too. But your safety comes first." A shuffling sounded over the airwaves. "I'm at the boat ramp now. It's been a while since I've used this one, but it looks to still be in good shape."

Summer paddled when she needed to steer clear of objects, but for the most part, she allowed the current to do the work.

"How much experience do you have kayaking?" Aiden's voice sounded calm and inviting.

"Just what I've been able to do since moving here

last August. My sister and I lived in New York after growing up in Washington, D.C. The closest thing I've done to this is sculling on the Potomac."

"That counts for experience on the water."

Summer shifted the phone from one ear to the other. "Are you trying to build my confidence again?"

"Is it working?"

"Maybe a little." She floated around a bend and the whitewater came into view. "Tell me again about these rapids."

"Keep to the left. There's a spot to the right that's easy to get sucked into a vortex."

"Vortex?" Summer swallowed as the first sprinkles of rain hit her bare shoulders and wind gusted. "That sounds ominous even without the storm brewing overhead."

"It can be tricky to handle when the river's flowing so fast."

The kayak picked up speed, bumping over the large ripples.

Summer paddled hard to keep left. She managed to avoid the swirling mass, but in her efforts, the paddle wedged against something deep beneath the surface. The handle tore from her grasp with a painful twist, and the paddle plopped into the water. "Oh, no…" She lunged to retrieve it and the kayak wobbled. Water rushed in, soaking her clothes and backpack. She stabilized herself, but not before the current carried the paddle beyond reach.

"Summer?" Aiden's voice grew urgent. "What is it?"

She grasped the cellphone tight; it was one of the only allies she had left. "You won't believe this."

"Try me."

"I lost the paddle."

"OK. Tell me what you've got with you in the boat." As if accustomed to unexpected complications, Aiden didn't miss a beat and his direct tone kept her focused.

Summer took inventory. "I have a backpack with a water bottle, some snacks, a hat, and my keys." She lifted her baseball cap, swiped aside perspiration and then resettled it on her head.

"All right. Can you secure your keys in your life preserver?"

She checked. "Yes, there's a zippered pocket on the front."

"Store the keys there."

She dug in her backpack and did as he asked. "Done." The kayak hit a protruding boulder, bounced off. Water sloshed around in the bottom, covering her water shoes. She teetered for a moment and then regained balance.

"Anything else valuable like an ID?"

Summer shook her head as if he could see her. "No. Why?"

"Because you're going to have to get in the water and swim, and you might have to let the kayak go."

"S-swim?" Her heart jolted. She scanned the river. Fallen branches, logs, and various debris swept alongside her. She could be hit by something, or be sucked into one of those whirlpools Aiden had mentioned. "I'd rather not get in there."

"You don't have a choice. There's a large hydroelectric dam a couple miles downriver. With the water flowing so rapidly, if you get too close, it could thrust you over the edge."

She'd seen that dam from land before. The ledge

had a huge drop on the other side, making it impossible to pass over safely. Her stomach turned queasy at the danger lying in wait. "OK. I'll get in the river and swim."

"Are you through the rapids yet?"

She'd bounced her way across most of the turbulence. "Almost. I've got about a hundred yards to go."

"Good. Do you see a fifty-foot-tall outcropping of rocks on the right bank?"

"Yes." Recognizing a landmark made her feel marginally better.

"When you are parallel with the rocks, get in the water and start swimming toward shore."

"All right. I've got a watertight bag with me. I'm going to put my phone in it. If I can't get to you—"

"Then I'll come after you. It's going to be all right. I'm not leaving here without you."

He'd better not. Not after all this. The outcropping came up fast, and with shaky fingers she cut off the phone, tucked it into the bag, and secured it along with the keys.

Lord, help me get to Aiden.

She grabbed the kayak's rope and climbed over the side. The cool water shocked overheated skin, soaking clothes. The added weight hindered her movements as she kicked toward shore. Water splashed into her mouth and she sputtered. The kayak tugged against her, but she held fast and used the craft to shield her from floating debris.

As she cleared the rocky outcropping, Aiden's black truck appeared. He had parked in a small gravel lot alongside the river.

Although the ramp itself looked well used, tall

grass and thick underbrush surrounded the area. If she hadn't been expecting the boat ramp, she probably would've missed it altogether. But there was zero chance she would've missed Aiden—he stood like a sentinel on the worn, narrow dock, his gaze scanning the river. He had already removed his shirt and boots, and as soon as he spotted her, he dove in.

With renewed purpose, she surged forward. The current forced the kayak downstream, and the attached rope dragged against her palm. Pain sliced through her hand but she kept hold—she hadn't come this far to give up now. Fighting to maintain her grip on the kayak, she pulled her free arm through the water and kicked her way toward shore.

With long, powerful strokes, Aiden met her halfway and grasped her arm with one hand and the kayak with the other. "Are you all right?"

She'd been soothed by his voice on the phone, but having him there in the flesh was much more rewarding. "Never been better."

His answering smile played havoc on her senses. "Let's get out of here." His strength outmatched hers considerably, and she welcomed the reprieve as he propelled them both toward shore. He kept a tight hold on the kayak as the current tugged at it. "You took a risk by keeping the boat with you."

Summer kicked alongside him. "Aren't you the one who said taking risks is the only way to find out if something's going to work?"

His smile widened. "Fair enough."

Summer touched the bottom and she sloshed her way up the ramp, goose bumps rising as the wind touched her wet skin. She helped Aiden drag the kayak onto shore, not at all surprised her legs shook in the process. She removed her dripping lifejacket, relieved to breathe freely again.

Aiden retrieved her backpack and handed it over. He hauled the kayak up and over his head, balancing the boat on his shoulders as he carried it toward the truck. His bicep muscles flexed with the heavy load.

"Impressive."

Aiden stumbled and dropped the kayak, barely managing to stay on his feet.

Oops. She hadn't meant to say that out loud. "Sorry. I didn't mean to distract you."

Recovering his balance, he glanced up. "Don't worry about it. It's not your fault I get nervous around you." He headed for the truck and grabbed his shirt and boots from the driver's side.

"I make you nervous?" More than a little self-conscious, she plucked at her clingy, wet clothes.

Aiden leaned against the truck and slipped on his boots. "You hadn't noticed?" His appreciative gaze flitted over her as he tied laces.

Summer's heart rate doubled. Electricity sparked in the air, and it had nothing to do with the approaching storm. "So that's why you've been avoiding me? I thought you didn't like me."

His brows drew together. "I'm sorry I gave you that impression."

A sudden clap of thunder pierced the air.

"You'd better get in. It's going to downpour any second now. I'll get the kayak loaded."

Summer deposited her backpack in the truck but didn't get inside. He'd helped her out of her predicament and she could help load the boat. She circled the truck, thankful for some time to digest what he'd said. If she made him nervous, then maybe there was something to her being drawn to him. Maybe the feeling was mutual. Heavy raindrops slapped her hat, shoulders, and everything else as the storm finally let loose. She approached Aiden as he pulled nylon rope from the truck's cab.

He looked up, and his eyes widened as if he was surprised she hadn't sought refuge.

She shrugged. "I'm already soaked. What can I do to help?"

Aiden handed over the rope. "Hold this a sec."

She took hold and their fingers brushed. The contact lasted much shorter of a time than when he'd held her arm in the water, but the impact was no less significant.

His gaze dipped to her lips and lingered.

A welcome shiver shot up her spine, and then as if he remembered they were getting pummeled with rain, Aiden released the truck's tailgate, hefted up the kayak, and slid it into the bed.

Summer handed over the rope.

He secured the kayak, looking more than capable of handling this and anything else that came his way. Even with water pouring over him, mud splashing up on his boots, and his blue eyes squinting against the onslaught, Summer had never seen a more appealing man.

Aiden caught her staring.

She struggled for something to say. "You look as if you've done this before."

"A time or two." He shrugged as if he'd finished something ordinary, like folding a load of laundry.

His humble attitude impressed her more than anything. "Whoever it is that had the honor of raising you did a fantastic job."

A smile played at his lips, and he stood a little straighter as he escorted her to the passenger side. He opened the door and she slid inside. Aiden's masculine scent lingered in the enclosed space and she closed her eyes a moment, enjoying the sense of security surrounding her.

The momentary quiet broke as Aiden opened the driver's side door. The car dipped with his weight as he settled into his seat. His pulse throbbed in a vein in his neck, showing his rapid heartbeat.

She shifted toward him. "I'm making you nervous again, aren't I?"

Vulnerability shone through his gaze. "I handle life-threatening situations almost daily, but the thought of asking you out and being rejected stops me cold."

Summer bit her lip to keep her mouth from dropping open. The part about him handling life-threatening situations on a routine basis sent up a red flag in her mind, but it was overshadowed by the rest of his admission. "All this time you've been avoiding me, you've wanted to ask me out?"

He gripped the steering wheel with both hands. "Sad, isn't it?"

"Actually, it's flattering." Summer's own nerves kicked in and she drew in a deep breath. "Just for the record, if you do ask me out, you won't have to worry about being rejected."

8

"She's fine, Dottie." Aiden stood in his neighbor's doorway, reassuring her. "Summer's back in her apartment, safe and sound."

"Oh, thank goodness." Dottie glanced over his wet clothes as Patches squirmed in her arms. "Is it raining that hard or did you take a swim?"

"Both. I helped Summer out of the river and then I got drenched again while tending to the boat." But he didn't care how sodden he'd become, the rescue had been a success in more ways than one. Summer was home again, and she had given him the green light to ask her out. The knowledge lifted his spirits. He only prayed he wouldn't botch everything up when the time came to do the asking.

"I knew you were the right man for the job. Let me get you a towel, and then you can tell me all about it."

He waited at the door while she retrieved a yellow hand towel. "Thanks." He ran the cloth over his hair, face, and along his neck.

"So tell me. Where did you find her?"

"The current had carried her several miles downriver. We met up at a boat ramp."

"You make it all sound so simple. But I know it was dangerous with all the extra water streaming from the mountains."

"That's why I'm glad I got her out of there." He'd participated in many rescues on the Shenandoah River, and some of them had turned into search and recovery missions. He couldn't stomach the thought of Summer becoming one of those statistics.

Dottie's eyes held understanding as she looked him over. "You must be cold."

"I do need to get dry clothes on." He finished wiping his exposed skin and knelt to clean the drips off the floor.

Patches sprang from Dottie's arms and climbed onto Aiden's knee. His little warm body heated Aiden's cool skin.

"It's good to see you, too."

Patches looked up, tail wagging, as if fully expecting Aiden to remain kneeling just for him.

"I can't stay and play this time, buddy, but I promise I'll be back sometime."

As if he understood, Patches barked once, hopped to the floor, and padded past Dottie into the apartment. He found his way to his food bowl, licking remnants as Aiden handed over the towel.

Dottie inched forward, as if reluctant to let him go. "I'm really glad to have a strong, handsome man for a neighbor. I'm sure Summer is too, especially now that you've come to her rescue." She paused. "Again."

Aiden's face heated. "You know about the door incident?"

"I finagled the info out of her. It would've been hard not to notice the clamps on the door that night."

"Yeah, well, busting into her apartment to find her unharmed doesn't actually count as a rescue." Aiden tucked his hands into his pockets.

"Summer didn't seem to mind." Dottie winked. "How was the cobbler she made for you?"

"I wouldn't know. I didn't get to taste it. We had a run-in of sorts and it didn't make it into a bowl. I'm hoping she'll make another one."

"Oh well. Maybe she will." Dottie waved a hand and leaned forward. "I drove Frank to the airport earlier today so he could catch his cruise, and he told me he has leased the last vacant apartment to a man named Dr. Devin Paxton. He's a pediatrician from Luray."

"Frank mentioned something about it." He'd also mentioned that the new neighbor would be bringing a dog with him, which could prove to be interesting with Patches and Tom already in the mix.

"Oh, I hope he's nice. You never know these days."

"Frank does a background check on his applicants, I'm sure everything will be fine." Although Aiden didn't want to be rude, the hallway's air-conditioning vent spewed out cold air and his damp clothes iced over. "I should get going."

"One more thing real quick." Dottie fiddled with a turquoise earring. "Are you, by any chance, participating in the bachelor auction?"

"I haven't made up my mind yet." But he needed to. The event was coming up this Saturday. "Why?"

"Because I won a ticket and gave it to Summer."

Aiden's heart skipped a beat. "She's going?"

Dottie lifted a shoulder and continued to play with her earring. "She accepted the ticket."

Aiden's breath caught in his lungs. If he joined the auction, she could bid on a date with him. That way, he wouldn't have to fumble his way through asking her out. But procuring a date with her when he was the only guy around was one thing, and it was another matter entirely when standing alongside a dozen or so other prospects. What if she bid on some other guy?

Still, he couldn't pass up the opportunity. "In that case, I'll be there."

Dottie clapped her hands together and gushed, "That's wonderful."

So, Dottie had a little matchmaking in mind. He was OK with that. As long as it involved him with Summer. He excused himself and headed toward his apartment. He had his cellphone in hand the moment he shut the door behind him.

Captain Warren answered on the second ring. "I hope you've called to tell me you'll support your local firefighters' auction?"

"You can count me in."

"That's what I wanted to hear. I'll add you to the list."

Anticipation began to build. "This should be interesting."

"No doubt." Captain Warren cleared his throat. "Oh, and, Aiden...the competition is fierce. Be prepared to take off your shirt."

9

Summer stood before her closet, contemplating what to wear to the auction. She rummaged through her clothes with one hand and held her cellphone to her ear with the other. "I can't believe I'm doing this."

"Oh, come on. Live a little," Riley encouraged.

"I have dressy clothes but they make me look like a schoolteacher."

"That's because you work at a school."

"So, what do you suggest?" Summer squeezed her eyes shut. She shouldn't have asked. Riley's sense of style reflected fashion trends, while comfort ruled Summer's choices.

"Wear something that shows off your legs. And don't forget high heels."

"Why? I'm not the one going up on stage." She continued pushing hangers around. "And don't forget where the auction is being held. I am in the country, you know."

"Fine. Then slap on some overalls, grab a straw hat, and you'll be good to go. Don't even bother with shoes. They're overrated anyway."

"Ha-ha. Very funny." Summer gave up and fell back onto her pillow-topped mattress. She twirled her ruby ring around her finger. "I guess I could wear a sundress. Maybe a necklace." She should be more worried about what she'd wear if Aiden asked her out. She'd hoped he would before leaving her at her door the other day, but he'd excused himself without mentioning anything. Then again, it hadn't been the best time. They'd both been tired and soaking wet.

"Seriously. Relax. Enjoy yourself. Maybe something great will come of this."

If only Riley knew of Summer's decision not to date men in dangerous professions. But she didn't want to bring that up. "I might not even bid on any of the guys anyway. I could just give a donation."

"Don't you dare," Riley admonished. "You deserve to find someone special."

"So do you." Summer squeezed her eyes shut. Riley had had that someone special and he'd left. Not by choice, but he'd left just the same. "I'm sorry."

"I know." Riley's supportive tone wavered. "But while we're on the subject, I have been thinking about what you said about Zack coming to stay with you for a while. Did you mean it?"

Summer sprang into a sitting position. She'd had time to think since she'd blurted out the offer, and the thought of becoming responsible for a rebellious teen made her dizzy. But Riley needed her. "Yes. I meant it."

"Good. Because I was thinking sending Zack to you might be for the best."

"Did something else happen?"

"It's more like a series of things. He stays out past curfew. Sometimes he doesn't come home at all, and he barely talks to me anymore."

"Is he willing to come?"

"I haven't talked to him about it yet."

Apprehension squeezed her chest tight. "You are going to tell him, right?"

"Well, I should."

"Riley. He has to agree to this or he won't stay."

Summer could imagine Zack catching a bus out of town and going to who-knows-where.

"Let me work on it. I'll call you in a few days."

"A few days would be fine." More than fine, actually. That would give her time to get used to the idea. "I'll talk to you soon."

"I don't know what I'd do without you." Riley's voice hitched and then silence fell.

Summer pulled the phone away from her ear and looked at the screen. Riley had disconnected. The conversation had put a lot of things into perspective. Her dilemma of what to wear to the auction paled in comparison to Riley's trials.

Closing her eyes, Summer bent her head and prayed. *Lord, help Riley and Zack know what's for the best. And, if Zack does agree to come here, help me be able to handle him.*

10

Summer's face had to be as red as the sundress she'd chosen to wear as bachelor number one leaned from the stage and handed her a rose.

Apparently, this man, introduced as Adam Thayer, had no problem showing off his assets. He worked the stage as if he had experience in this sort of thing, moving to the rhythm of the pulse-pounding music and garnering cheers and shouts from the audience. With the lights dimmed and a spotlight following his every move, the atmosphere sizzled with an excitement that unnerved Summer.

The fire engines had been moved outside, and the large room was filled with at least a hundred folding chairs, which were ignored by dozens of women rushing the stage. Some screamed and waved their auction paddles in the air as the bidding began, while others tried to get a peek at the next bachelor up, still hidden behind a wide curtain.

Summer hadn't known what to expect, but this was not it. She knew the event was a benefit for the fire department, but...wow! And who knew there were so many single women within range of three counties? And with the tickets priced at over a hundred dollars each, she hadn't expected quite this turnout.

"Having fun yet?"

Summer turned at the familiar voice.

Dottie took the seat next to her, grinning from ear to ear. "What did I miss?" She looked at the bachelor on stage and waved her paddle.

"Wait a minute." Summer leaned close and shouted above the noise. "You gave me your ticket. What are you doing here?"

"You didn't think I was going to miss out on all the fun, did you?" Dottie's smile pushed up the wrinkles on her face. "I bought my own ticket."

"Miss out? I thought you gave me your ticket because you didn't want to come?"

Dottie's reply was drowned out by shouts and catcalls as the bidding reached a frenzied level.

"Two hundred fifty!" Dottie shouted.

Adam danced close, winked at Dottie, and then pranced away.

"Do you know him?"

"I know most of the guys. Aside from bingo, I attend various functions throughout the year. Fundraisers. Picnics. Bake sales. Barbeques. That sort of thing. They're all kind of like family."

"I see. And did you give me this ticket with any particular firefighter in mind?"

Dottie gave an innocent shrug and returned her focus to the stage.

Summer's already nervous stomach fluttered. "Well, you'd better tell me who so I don't miss him."

"Don't worry, dear." Dottie waved a hand absently. "You'll know as soon as you see him."

Summer sat in a slight daze as the bidding for Adam ended. For a whopping four hundred twenty-five dollars, a young brunette secured herself a night on the town with the handsome, if not a bit flashy, bachelor number one.

Next up, a red-headed man walked across the stage, fully dressed in firefighting gear. The auctioneer didn't have time to introduce him before the music started and the women went wild. He chucked off his helmet and coat in time with the music. Summer zeroed in on Dottie. "This is so not how I pictured this."

"Relax. It's for a good cause." Dottie tossed up her hand, starting the bid at fifty dollars.

Summer sighed and settled in for the duration.

Dottie soon lost the bidding war, and the date with this hunk was sold for over three hundred dollars.

"Drat." Dottie folded her arms across her chest but her smile remained. She turned to Summer. "Oh well, the best is yet to come."

Summer let her lips quirk the slightest bit. Everything she'd seen so far had been good natured and PG-rated, and both the women and men seemed to be enjoying themselves. Before long, she found herself looking forward to seeing who was next in line, but as the evening progressed, a certain dark-haired neighbor kept popping into her mind as the date she really wanted.

For now, she had come, so she figured she needed to participate at some point. When an attractive, brown-haired guy edged onto the stage with a blush on his cheeks that reached all the way to the tips of his ears, Summer took notice. He wasn't like the others in their brazen attempts to garner attention. This one looked to be reserved.

The auctioneer stepped beside the guy. "Ladies, hang on to your hearts. Bryce Stolz has a soft spot for animals and volunteers at the local shelter."

"Aww." A collective sigh resounded in the room.

Encouraged, Bryce lifted his head, looked into the crowd, and smiled. Dimples appeared on his flushed cheeks and the bidding war began.

He seemed as good a guy as any. And he liked animals. Summer lifted her auction paddle at the hundred dollar mark, but before the auctioneer could acknowledge her bid, Dottie grabbed Summer's wrist and yanked it down.

"Not that one."

"Why not?" Summer didn't see anything wrong with him. She could handle one date with the guy to support the charity fund.

"Trust me. He's not the one you want."

Summer lifted a brow but Dottie didn't look at her to see her questioning gaze. What on earth did the woman have in mind?

An enthusiastic lady in the crowd bid over seven hundred dollars for Bryce Stolz, securing the date amongst an astonished crowd. The woman strode toward the stage, crooked a finger at Bryce.

He leaned down and she planted a firm kiss on his lips.

Applause deafened Summer as the women cheered, the excitement in the room reaching an all-time high. Caught up in the festive atmosphere, Summer finally allowed herself to relax.

Dottie nudged her. "I told you this would be fun."

She grinned. "Yes. You did."

"Next up in our line of heroes, we have a man of faith, integrity, and honor," the auctioneer announced as he reined in the crowd. "A man who has received the most prestigious Valor Award for risking his life to save an infant."

Dottie leaned close. "Sounds like a winner to me."

Summer's interest piqued, and she nodded her agreement but kept her gaze on the stage.

The auctioneer took a step back, held out a hand toward the curtain. "Ladies, let's have a round of applause for Glade Springs's very own Aiden Hawk."

Summer gasped as Aiden stepped onto the stage. Her sometimes shy neighbor was a firefighter? The rose slipped from numb fingers and the auction paddle clattered to the floor. Bidding on a stranger for charity was one thing; bidding on someone she would like to have in her life for much more than one obligatory date was another matter entirely.

Aiden Hawk was officially off limits. At least for her. The crowd exploded with cheers and the auctioneer set the starting bid at two hundred dollars. Women shouted and raised their paddles as Summer slipped from her chair and dashed toward the exit.

11

Summer inhaled the warm night air, but the humidity lay so heavy it did little to clear her mind. Ever since Aiden admitted he wanted to date her, she'd allowed herself to believe they could share something special.

So much for that idea.

Disappointment weighed on her shoulders, making every step an effort. She made it to her SUV moments before a torrent of rain let loose. She flipped on the windshield wipers and drove toward The Meadows, straining to see through low visibility.

Self-preservation was essential, right? So why did shame plague her? Sitting in the front row had prevented a stealthy getaway. What must Aiden think about her hasty retreat?

Rain pelted her windshield and she set her headlights to high beam. The shaking in her hands didn't help to steady the wheel, so when her cellphone rang, she ignored it. The call could wait. Determined to concentrate on only her driving, she focused on the road. She'd get home and then contemplate the evening's events.

As the town's streetlights ended, Summer slowed and leaned toward the steering wheel as if the extra couple of inches would help her see better. It didn't. She'd have to pull over somewhere until the rain let up, or she might—

A car rounded the corner with blinding

headlights.

The sudden change in visibility threw her off—she could no longer see the road. Summer slammed on the brakes. Her SUV hydroplaned, hit the muddy, rain-soaked shoulder, and slid sideways. A scream tore from her throat as the back end dipped over a steep embankment, leaving the vehicle teetering on a precipice above an overflowing stream. Summer pressed the accelerator, but rear tires found no traction.

Willing the car to stabilize, Summer eased off the pedal and held her breath. Agonizing seconds passed, and then with a sickening groan the SUV rolled backward, tumbling upside down into the stream.

Summer's head slammed against the driver's side window and searing pain erupted. The seatbelt choked her as it tightened around her abdomen and shoulders. She hung suspended as water rushed past her windows, bubbling and swirling with unimaginable force. Then, it seeped into the car. The dashboard lights flickered and then the faint glow went out, leaving her in total darkness.

Lord, help me.

~*~

Aiden prayed for an end to what had become his worst nightmare. Before the auction had begun, he'd had high hopes Summer would win a date with him, but his optimism had been crushed the moment she ran for the door. Now he was left with various women fighting over him, not because of who he was, but because of what he did for a living. He was a piece of meat, hunted by a gaggle of carnivores.

This was supposed to be fun?

"Take it all off," a woman taunted.

Not going to happen. He'd dated women who looked to his outward appearance and chosen profession as a standard. Summer was different. In fact, she'd responded to him better before she'd known he was a firefighter.

"One thousand dollars." Dottie's voice sounded above all the others.

God bless the woman for trying to save him. He motioned to the auctioneer to cut the bidding off, but the man refused to comply.

"Do we have eleven-hundred?" He continued in typical auction style, rambling so fast Aiden could hardly understand.

A woman up front outbid Dottie.

His stomach sank. What had he gotten himself into?

Dottie bid again, raising the stakes another hundred.

The bidding continued. Hands flew into the air, paddles waved.

Just when he resigned himself to the prolonged torture, the fire station's alarm sounded, disrupting the chaos. Aiden sprang into action, at once relieved by the interruption and concerned that someone had called in an emergency. He darted through the crowd, his focus zoned in on Captain Warren. "Where are we headed?" He stepped into his boots and yanked up his turnout gear.

Captain Warren readied himself. "A single vehicle accident alongside River Road."

Unease crept along Aiden's spine. Summer had left moments ago. But it couldn't be her. Could it?

Captain Warren, Aiden, and several others

climbed into Engine 11. Mike, the engineer, flipped on the sirens and they headed out.

Aiden's unease soon turned into a sense of foreboding. Summer would've had to travel along River Road to return to The Meadows. It was dark. Raining. No. He wouldn't go there. What were the odds something had happened to her anyway? He shook his head. Just because she'd been upset when she left...the sinking feeling returned. Deeper this time. *Lord, let Your guiding hand be on this situation.*

They rounded a bend and arrived at the accident scene.

Aiden's breath lodged in his throat; Summer's SUV lay upside down in a stream.

Drowning.

12

Summer fought dizziness, and her head throbbed. She could pass out. She might have already. The water level had risen several inches. She had to escape. Struggling with the seatbelt, Summer pushed desperately at the stubborn latch. After several attempts, the belt finally released. She braced herself the best she could for the fall, but her head hit the car's roof with force. She fell onto her side and struggled to sit upright as she sloshed around in the cold water.

With no light whatsoever, she fought to gain her bearings. She found the door and tried the power windows. They didn't move. She fumbled open the lock, pulled the door's handle, and shoved, but it wouldn't budge. The water's force outside her car had become her greatest enemy; the water inside her greatest nightmare. She couldn't die. Not here. Not now.

Riley needed her. Zack needed her. And Aiden...she hadn't had a chance to explain.

A flash of light caught her attention. But she had to have imagined it. She was alone. In the darkness. Unless the driver of that car she had passed witnessed her accident and had called for help. Hope emerged past paralyzing fears. Maybe she hadn't imagined the light. There it was again. A flashlight beam hit the windshield. Did she hear a voice? Yes. More than one. Calling her name. She squeezed her eyes shut. *Thank You, Lord.*

The windshield shattered and water rushed in, forcing Summer into the back. Her startled cry died in her throat as water filled the remaining space in the car. She slammed into seats, doors, and who knew what else.

Then, hands grabbed her. Tugging. Pulling her to safety.

When she broke through the water's surface, she sucked in fresh air.

Emergency lights flashed, men yelled.

Rain pelted her face.

Strong arms held her against a sturdy chest.

She blinked. Everything was fuzzy. Unfocused. But she could breathe freely, and she gave in to the urge to let herself fall into oblivion.

Too soon, something jostled her.

"Summer. Come back to me," a familiar voice beckoned.

She'd been moved into an ambulance and rain no longer assaulted her. Her entire body shivered, but she no longer felt cold. Gentle fingers lifted her eyelids. Bright light sought her pupils. She turned away. Her head pounded. Nausea rose.

Something compressed her arm. "Blood pressure's ninety over sixty." A woman's voice this time.

"Summer. Talk to me." The deep voice sounded again with more urgency than before. A soft blanket wrapped around her.

"Aiden?" She peeled open her eyes, and his handsome face came into view. Water dripped from his hair and fell onto his already saturated clothes. His warm hand folded over hers.

"It's me." He leaned close, concern creasing his brow. "Are you faint or dizzy?"

"I'm a little nauseous." She focused on his blue eyes and his gentle touch, letting everything and everyone else turn into a blur. "How did you know to come?"

"A witness called 911. We got here just in time."

If not for the straps securing her to a gurney, she would've launched into his arms. As it was, she managed a slight smile. "You have a tendency to do that."

He shrugged, but there was nothing casual about the gesture. "It's what I do."

Yes. She now had firsthand knowledge of what he did for a living. She should let his hand go, shield herself from becoming attached. But he kept her grounded when her entire world spun out of control.

A tow truck arrived and more sirens sounded.

"Do I have to go to the hospital?"

"Yes. It would be best."

Her pulse kicked up speed. "I don't like hospitals."

"Easy." Aiden brushed a kiss on her forehead. "I'll come with you."

"Can you?" Her voice cracked. "I mean. Are you allowed to?"

"It's not protocol, but this isn't a normal situation. I'm not leaving you."

Comforted, Summer allowed her eyes to drift shut.

"I know you want to sleep, but I need you to stay awake for me."

"I understand." But sleep called to her. It would be so easy to drift off.

The medic shut the door and the ambulance rolled away, sirens blaring.

Summer tensed and forced open her eyes. "My

purse is in my SUV."

"We'll look for your things after we get the vehicle out of the water." He kept his gaze glued to hers, as if he could will her to remain alert.

"You keep saying 'we.' You're a close-knit group, aren't you? You and the other firefighters and rescue workers."

"Yes. They're like family. Speaking of family, is there anyone you want me to call?"

Riley would want to know, but then she'd only worry. "I have a sister, but I can call her later."

"How about your parents?"

"If you call them, they would freak out. I love them, but I don't want them rushing here because of me. They have too much going on in D.C."

Aiden smoothed a thumb along the back of her hand. "What do they do?"

"Do you really want to know or are you trying to keep me talking?"

His smile did something quirky to her insides. "Both."

"Dad's into politics. Mom follows along for the fun of it, I guess. They're working on campaign projects. They love it."

"I'm guessing you're not too involved?"

"Not any more than I have to be." Talking sapped her energy and she lapsed into silence.

The medical technician checked her blood pressure again.

Aiden glanced at the woman. "How's she doing?"

"Better. Pressure's rising. It's one-ten over seventy."

The numbers didn't mean much to her, but Aiden's features relaxed a smidgeon.

"What do you think they'll do to me?"

"Run a couple of tests. Probably a CT scan."

Summer understood the need, but she didn't have to like it. The accident should never have happened in the first place. "It was raining so hard. I was looking for a place to pull over, but before I could find one…"

He tucked the blanket closer around her shoulders. "You skidded for quite a ways. It's a blessing you made it out alive."

Divine providence. She breathed another thankful prayer. She was just glad Aiden didn't ask why she'd rushed out of the auction. She could explain later. She let her eyes drift closed again.

"Summer. Stay with me."

It was difficult, but she looked at him. "I'm here."

"Don't scare me like this again. OK?"

She managed a weak smile. "No promises."

~*~

Aiden sat in the hospital's waiting area with a new appreciation for victims' family members. Waiting for test results on someone he cared about was torture. In the past few days, his fascination with Summer had grown exponentially. Falling in love with her would be easy and possibly inevitable if given enough time. But before he allowed himself to entertain the possibility, he would have to uncover why all this happened in the first place. She wouldn't have been in an accident if she hadn't fled from the auction.

When the emergency call had come in, he'd been more than ready and willing to respond. When his team had arrived on scene and he'd seen Summer's vehicle submerged in the water, he'd only had time to react on instincts and training. He'd done what he needed to do to get her out, but now that he had time to think, the gravity of the situation weighed on him.

She'd come too close to losing her life.

Aiden shivered and pulled a hand down his face. Maybe he'd be better off not thinking about such things. She would be fine. She had to be.

She'd not called her parents or her sister, even when she'd perked up a little. He'd been surprised when she signed the privacy papers that allowed him to know her prognosis.

He stood and paced the waiting room until the ER doctor emerged. "How is she?"

The petite woman produced a hurried smile. "Summer has a few bumps and bruises, but aside from that, nothing concerning."

"No concussion?"

"No. She will be sore for a few days though. Ibuprofen should work fine. I'm assuming you'll be able to get her home safely?"

"Of course." He'd arranged for the guys at the station to drop off his truck in the parking lot. They'd been able to retrieve Summer's belongings from her vehicle, and now with the go-ahead from the doctor, he was anxious to take her home.

Aiden shook the woman's hand and glanced at her name tag. "Thank you, Dr. Holston. Can I see her now?"

"Come with me." Dr. Holston led the way through busy corridors, past various equipment and nursing stations. She pulled aside a curtain and stepped away.

Summer lay on a hospital bed, pale skinned, with eyes red-rimmed as if she'd been crying, but the IV had been removed and she'd already changed into the sweatshirt and pants he had picked up at a nearby store.

Aiden's heart shifted, but he mustered an optimistic smile. "Hey there. How are you feeling?"

"I've had enough of the water for a while. But other than that, I'm fine and dandy."

"I'd be lying if I said you looked fine and dandy."

She winced, but smiled. "I appreciate the honesty."

Aiden crossed his arms and propped a hip on the bed. "Doc says you're ready to go. Do you have discharge papers yet?"

"Yes. But I don't have a car."

"I'll drive you."

"You've done so much already. Saving my life." Summer waved a hand. "Sticking around while I got poked and prodded with needles, machines, and all kinds of gadgets. You must've been bored out of your mind."

"Nothing involving you is boring." Aiden leaned forward. "Besides, rescuing people is my job."

"Yeah, about that…" She clasped hands on her lap and twisted a red gemstone ring on her finger as she averted her gaze.

Aiden stiffened, unsure where the conversation was heading, but he suspected it had something to do with why she had high-tailed it away from the auction.

Finally, when she looked up, tears glistened. "I wish things could be different."

His stomach plunged, not for the first time tonight, and he had a sinking feeling he knew what was coming.

13

"So, the other day I told Aiden how I feel about dating men in dangerous careers." Summer sat on the dock, holding Patches and dipping her toes in the Shenandoah River. "Do you know what he said?"

Patches looked up with adoring eyes, listening to every word of the one-sided conversation. He tilted his head as if eager to hear more.

Summer leaned close to his ear and whispered, "He used the *f* word."

Patches licked her hand as if in sympathy.

"I know, right? Can you believe he offered to be *friends*?" She hugged Patches closer. "How many guys do you know willingly take the friendship route after being rejected? Especially after being told they wouldn't be rejected?" A pang of regret hit her.

He'd looked so disappointed when she told him.

Patches laid his head in her lap and sighed.

"Aiden was so gracious about it all. As if he completely understood." She rubbed Patches. "I thought it was a guy's worst nightmare to have a woman they want to date use the *f* word on them. And Aiden used the *f* word on me first."

Could she be just friends with someone she was so attracted to?

Summer lifted her legs, flinging water with her toes. The quick movement awakened sore muscles. The accident had taken its toll, but at least her headache had eased.

She adjusted her sunglasses, glad the rain had cleared and opened up bright blue skies. "You and Aiden are the only ones I've told about my fears of risky jobs."

She couldn't tell Riley. Not yet, at least. And talking it over with her parents would be a disaster. Mom would insist she see a therapist.

"Good thing I have you, sweetheart."

Patches perked up as a stick floated past. She grasped his collar tight to make sure he didn't plunge in after the moving object. He stood and pranced on her lap, trying to get at it anyway. Oh, the life of a dog.

Summer smiled and shook her head. If only she could be entertained by such small things.

Patches suddenly turned his head and barked.

"What is it?"

A vehicle's tires crunched along the winding driveway. Her pulse went into overdrive. Aiden? She hadn't seen him since he'd brought her home after the accident. She wanted to make certain he wouldn't start avoiding her again. But the rumbles coming from the vehicle weren't deep and masculine like Aiden's truck. This engine had a more sophisticated sound, like the soft purr of a cat.

A silver convertible pulled into the spot Aiden normally used. A well-dressed, handsome blond guy looking to be in his early to mid-thirties stepped out carrying a dog about the same size as Patches.

Patches tore out of her grasp. He bounded across the yard, aiming for the new arrival.

The other animal started barking and leapt from its owner's arms. It ran toward Patches. Certain the two would meet in a head-on collision, Summer jumped to her feet and ran.

The man rounded the car. "Zoe. Come back."

Summer regretted her impulsive move as the headache she'd recently rid herself of returned. She forced her steps to slow. "Patches. Come on, boy."

The two dogs stopped within a few feet of each other, circled, and began sniffing. Although they were both Chihuahuas, the dogs looked nothing alike. While Patches was long-haired and covered in beige and white fur, Zoe had a short solid brown coating.

Zoe's owner stopped a few feet away. "It's good to see she will have a playmate."

Summer digested what he'd said. "Playmate? Oh, you must be the new tenant."

He smiled, showing a set of perfect teeth. He held out a hand. "Dr. Devin Paxton, Apartment 2D."

She took his offered greeting. "Summer Cassel. Apartment 2A."

Zoe looked up, saw their joined hands, and began a barking marathon. The dog abandoned her post next to Patches and tore up grass on her way to nip at Summer's heels.

Razor-sharp teeth connected with Summer's ankle and pain erupted.

Dr. Paxton scooped up Zoe before she could cause further damage. "I'm so sorry. Are you OK?"

Summer checked her injury. The little animal had drawn blood, but considering the accident she'd survived on Saturday night, yeah, she was fine. "I'll live." She was determined not to start out on the wrong foot with this neighbor. "Zoe probably thought she was protecting you."

Dr. Paxton deposited Zoe onto the convertible's passenger seat. "You don't look so dangerous to me." He flashed a quick smile. But his smile faded as he glanced at her ankle. "You're bleeding." He opened his trunk and withdrew a black bag, similar to those Summer had seen on old TV shows where the doctor made house calls. After closing the trunk, Dr. Paxton patted the top. "Hop on. Let me take a look."

"I'll be fine." Summer picked up Patches, cuddling him to her chest.

"I insist. Tending to your wound is the least I can do since it was my dog that hurt you."

True, but did she want a man she just met touching her feet? Seemed intimate, all things considered. She was about to refuse again when he stepped toward her, took her by the waist, and hefted her up to sit on the trunk.

"Oh." The warmth from the car heated her backside, while another kind of warmth crept up her cheeks. In all that had happened, she hadn't noticed the guy's impressive biceps. Muscles bulged under his button-down dress shirt, and trousers covered what looked to be athletic legs. Overall, Dr. Paxton was quite attractive. His spicy cologne might've even held a certain appeal, if it hadn't made her nose itch.

After releasing her, he kept a respectable distance as he dug into his bag. "So, how did you get the bruises on your forehead?"

Summer touched fingertips to the sore area. "Car accident." She was just getting to the point where she could talk about it without shivering, which was a marked improvement from when she'd called Riley and told her. During that conversation, she'd broken into a cold sweat.

Concern creased Dr. Paxton's brow as he studied her bruise, and he looked tempted to pull out a pen light and check her pupil's dilation.

She'd better keep him focused on one thing at a time, or he'd have her back in the hospital for a full work-up. "I think the bleeding has stopped." Of course, she hadn't actually looked at her ankle again, so she had no way of knowing if that was true.

Summer scooted forward to get off the car, but Dr. Paxton took up her heel in his palm before she could make good her escape.

His hand felt warm with underlying strength like Aiden's, but where calluses lined Aiden's skin, Dr. Paxton's felt like silk. The distinction between the two was remarkable. And, so was her reaction. This guy's touch didn't have any significant impact. But she really had no right to compare the two men. She didn't know that much more about Aiden than she did Dr. Paxton. The auction had proven that. If she'd known Aiden was a firefighter from the beginning…she would've what? Not spoken to him? Not made a cobbler? Not allowed him to rescue her from the river or the car? Summer shook her head. She would've done all those things. The only difference would've been that she'd have never considered dating him.

"How long have you lived here?" Dr. Paxton smoothed an antiseptic wipe across the wound.

The resulting sting made her jump and jolted her from her musings. "Almost a year."

He nodded. "I hope it's as peaceful as it appears."

She relaxed with the small talk. "It is, unless you get caught on the river in a thunderstorm." Or have your car flip upside down into an overflowing stream. But she kept that little tidbit to herself.

"You won't catch me on the water. I prefer indoor activities. Theatre. Symphonies. That sort of thing."

"Then why did you want to move way out here?

Aside from hiking, canoeing, and kayaking, bingo is the favorite pastime for most folks in Glade Springs. Not plays and operas."

"I wanted a quiet place to call home after a long day at work. I found there were too many distractions in town. Way too many kids in my neighborhood."

"Wait. I thought you were a pediatrician?"

He paused and met her gaze. "I am, but I'd rather not take my work home with me."

"I see." So, the good doctor had some not-so-appealing side effects. What kind of pediatrician wanted to avoid kids after hours? She attempted to retrieve her foot.

Dr. Paxton held firm. "Not what you expected to hear, is it? Don't get me wrong. I do love kids. It's...well...it's more of the parents who are the issue. I rarely have an evening where I don't get a knock on my door from someone looking for a diagnosis. I rarely get a full night's sleep. I'm hoping moving here will change that."

His explanation sounded reasonable enough, and shame filled her for thinking the worst. "Well, welcome to The Meadows. I think you'll find it nice and quiet here." She thought of the night Tom cat had joined her and Patches. "Well, for the most part anyway."

Dr. Paxton resumed his work on her injury.

She tried not to flinch as he secured a bandage on her ankle.

The distinctive, throaty sound of Aiden's truck caught Summer's attention. As the rumbling grew closer, her heart beat faster. Although Frank had not assigned specific parking spots to his tenants, Summer had come to think of this one as Aiden's.

Would he mind that the new neighbor had parked here?

Aiden's truck rounded the last bend in the driveway and he slowed before turning in beside Dr. Paxton's convertible. He parked, slid out, and pinned her with a gaze mixed with concern and curiosity. "Everything OK?"

Zoe, who had just calmed, started in on another barking frenzy.

Patches joined in creating so much noise no one could talk.

Aiden stepped close, bringing with him a fresh-out-of-the-shower scent. His hair glistened in the morning light, as if he'd recently cleaned up after his shift.

She stopped herself before leaning toward him for closer inspection.

Friends. They were *just* friends.

Aiden rubbed Patches under his chin, but kept a wary gaze on Dr. Paxton.

Patches quieted and started licking. Zoe took the hint and settled as well.

The two men sized each other up but said nothing.

Summer remembered her manners. "Dr. Paxton. This is Aiden Hawk. Apartment 2B. Aiden, this is the pediatrician Frank spoke of."

The men shook hands and then Dr. Paxton turned his attention to Summer. "All things considered, I think we've gotten past formalities." He lifted her foot for emphasis. "Call me Devin."

Summer could've imagined it, but she thought Aiden's muscles tensed. She glanced up. No. She hadn't imagined anything. A muscle in his jaw twitched.

"What happened?" Aiden's palm found its way to the small of her back. With his other hand still on Patches, he had her virtually surrounded. Or shielded from whatever threat he might think the doctor presented.

"Apparently I have unique ways of meeting my neighbors." Summer offered the explanation, detailing everything leading up to and including the ankle nip. "Devin is about finished doctoring the wound." She hoped. The longer her foot stayed in the man's hand, the more awkward the moment became.

Devin divided quick glances between Aiden and Summer. He released her ankle. "Sorry. Frank didn't tell me you two were a couple."

Oh, yeah. The awkward moment intensified. Aiden looked at her as if he wanted Devin's assumption to be true, which in turn triggered her own sense of longing. But she refused to nurture the sensation. Summer dragged away her gaze. If she lingered too long in his mesmerizing eyes, her resolve might slip. She somehow found her voice. "Aiden and I are—"

"Just friends," he finished for her but made no move to physically distance himself.

Devin nodded, gathered his things into his bag. "Well, I apologize again for Zoe's behavior. I'd like to make it up to you—"

"You've done more than enough already." Aiden's quick answer took Summer by surprise. "I'll take it from here." He wrapped one arm around her waist and the other under her legs, scooping both her and Patches off the car. He headed toward the apartment building, carrying her as if she weighed nothing.

"It was nice meeting you," Summer called over

Aiden's shoulder. Then in a quieter voice she asked, "What are you doing?" Not that she minded being held in his strong arms. The pressure of his hard chest against her shoulder gave her a sense of security. He smelled good too. She made a conscious effort not to turn her head and sniff his neck.

"I'm saving you from wasting six months of your life."

"What?"

Aiden stepped up on the porch, pushed open the door as Patches remained content in Summer's arms. "The neighborly doctor who just had his hands on your foot—for way longer than necessary—wants to do more than apologize."

"And how do you know this?"

Aiden crossed the foyer, heading for the stairs. "I know his type."

"And what type is that?"

"The type to sample as many women as he can fit into his busy schedule. He doesn't want to settle down. And raising a family...well, that won't happen."

It didn't matter to her one way or another. "Even if you are right, and I'm not saying that you are, what does this have to do with me?"

"He will ask you out. If you say yes, he'll act like a considerate gentleman. One date will lead to another." Aiden approached her door and gently set her on her feet. "Next thing you know, you'll have fallen for his charms only to discover he's not interested in commitment."

"And by whisking me away, you've saved me from certain heartbreak."

"Exactly."

"Then I suppose I should thank you."

"What can I say?" He smiled, tucking hands into pockets. "That's what friends are for."

"Then it's a good thing I have you." She quirked a brow. "Right?"

"Don't believe me? Wait and see. Within twenty-four hours, he'll show up with flowers. A dozen…no…two dozen roses. He'll apologize again for his dog's behavior. Then he'll ask you out to dinner. Maybe a moonlit stroll under the stars."

"You know, for a guy who hardly said more than two words to me for the first three weeks you lived here, you sure do have a lot to say now."

"Well, now that I know we're just friends, the pressure is off." His smile widened. "I can speak my mind without fear of saying something wrong and scaring you away."

Ah, so that was the key. "The silver lining of friendship." She grinned, enjoying the easy banter. "Don't worry. I've recently survived a run-in with Tom cat, a raging river, a terrifying car accident, and an attack from a high-strung little dog. I think I can handle our new neighbor. No matter how friendly he tries to be."

Aiden's smile slipped away and he stepped closer. "Seriously. Be careful. I don't want anyone hurting you."

"Don't you think you're overreacting a little?"

"Not when it comes to you."

"Oh." She stared into his fabulous, compassionate blue eyes. Believing his motives were honest and heartfelt, his protective streak warmed her rather than offended. "I will be careful," she whispered, blessed beyond measure to have him in her life, even if their relationship could never pass beyond friendship.

Now, why was that again?

As her gaze travelled along his perfect nose, darted over his angular jaw, and finally landed on lips just the right size for kissing, she struggled to remember her reasoning.

Aiden straightened and cleared his throat. "I'd better get going. I have a lot to do before my date tonight."

His words jolted her from her wayward thoughts. "Wait a minute. You've been warning me away from dating Dr. Paxton, and now you tell me *you're* going on a date? That's a double standard."

"Not really."

"How do you figure?" Summer planted hands on hips.

"My date doesn't have ulterior motives. She's from the bachelor auction."

"Oh. That was quick." Not even long enough for the check to clear. "Must be some kind of woman to get you to go out so fast."

"She is."

Unwarranted jealousy pricked her like a blackberry thorn, with a sharp sting that was sure to linger long after the initial contact. "I'd better let you get going, then. I'll see you later." Summer forced a smile and swept into her apartment. If she couldn't get a better handle on things, drawing the line at friendship might prove harder than she'd anticipated.

14

Summer pushed open the French doors, careful to keep an eye out for Tom cat. Even though Frank had left for vacation, Dottie had offered to feed Tom and often let him outside for fresh air.

Patches followed at Summer's heels. Apparently, Dottie had something pressing on her agenda because when she'd dropped Patches off, she'd been brimming with excitement.

"Well, looks like it's just you and me, Patchy Pooh." Summer sat on one of two deck chairs, propped her feet on the railing, and checked her cellphone for messages. She had missed a call from Riley while she'd been speaking with Aiden earlier, and she and Riley had been playing phone tag over the past several hours.

No calls showed on the screen. Summer sighed and tucked her phone in her pocket, intent on enjoying the view. The evening air had cooled to a comfortable level, and although dark clouds formed in the distance and thunder rumbled, the setting sun cast a rich variety of silver, gray, and pink hues across the horizon.

Patches sniffed the air, turned, and trotted inside.

Summer twisted around. "Hey. You're supposed to keep me company."

Patches hopped onto the couch and settled in for a nap. He grinned—the little traitor—and closed his eyes.

Summer shook her head, stood, and leaned against the waist-high railing. A couple of fishermen in a boat floated downriver and she waved. The two men returned her greeting. Then, irony struck. While Aiden was preparing for his date, her brief interaction with the passersby might very well turn out to be the social highlight of her evening.

A moment later, Aiden stepped onto his balcony while adjusting a patterned tie around his neck. He wore a pair of dark dress pants, a pale blue button-down shirt, and had two jackets tucked in his arms.

"Wow. Look at you." Summer crossed her balcony, bringing her a few feet closer.

Aiden spun to face her and grinned. "I'm not used to ties." He fought with the adjustments.

"Take it off."

"You think I should?"

"Yes. And unbutton the top button of your shirt."

He hesitated and then removed the tie and released the button. "Better?"

Her pulse leapt and her palms dampened. She swallowed. "Yeah. Better. Which jacket are you going to wear?"

"I don't know. What do you think?" He held up a dark formal jacket and a shade lighter sports jacket.

"The sports jacket. The other looks like you're trying too hard."

Aiden slipped on the one she chose, turned in a circle, and faced her again. "Good enough for a twelve-hundred-dollar date?" He flashed a bright smile.

Her mouth dried. She would've paid a thousand more just to see him smile like that again. She managed a nonchalant shrug. "It'll do."

As if satisfied, he headed for the door but stopped

short of returning inside. "How's your ankle?"

She hadn't thought much about it since the pain was only temporary. "Much better."

"Good. I'd rather the doctor not have an excuse to latch onto you again." He disappeared inside.

Summer's breath caught in her lungs. Had he been jealous? Before she could overanalyze his words, as she had a tendency to do, her cellphone rang. Riley. She cleared her throat and answered. "I thought we'd never catch up."

"Sorry. I've been in and out of meetings all day."

With one last glance toward Aiden's balcony, Summer returned inside and secured the French doors. "I was worried. When you called earlier and left a message, you sounded upset."

"Can you take Zack in this weekend? Or are you still recovering from the accident?"

"I'm feeling better." But if Zack were to come, she'd have to get her spare bedroom ready. The extra boxes she'd yet to unpack still covered the twin bed. She also had virtually nothing for a teenager to do, aside from having Internet connection. And food? She doubted Zack would be satisfied with living on yogurt, granola bars, and salads. But she could handle it. Right? "This weekend would be fine."

"You don't sound so sure."

"It'll be great. I've missed him. I've missed you both."

"He's changed, Summer. It's not like when you could take him out for ice cream and to feed the ducks at the park."

"I understand." She'd have to figure out what to do with him. Riley needed her. "Do you want me to come get him or do you want to bring him here?"

"I'd like to see where you live, so I'll drive him." Riley's voice hitched. "You know if I had other options, I wouldn't ask you to do this."

"We'll be fine."

"You don't really know what you're getting into."

"I know."

"It's going to be difficult."

"Are you trying to talk me out of it?"

Riley exhaled a deep breath. "No. I'm trying to talk *me* out of it. He's my life."

So, Riley was placing her world in Summer's hands. No pressure. "I'll need to know what your rules are. Curfews, that sort of thing."

"I can tell you what my rules are, but when he's with you, you'll have to set your own boundaries. Now, whether he chooses to listen, that's another thing altogether."

Summer's heart raced. Riley was liable to scare Summer into retracting her offer. She'd better get off the phone before she chickened out. "How about if we talk more later?"

"OK. I owe you."

"No, you don't. This is what sisters are for. See you soon." Summer disconnected as a boatload of things she'd have to get done came to mind.

She hadn't gotten around to renting a car yet. She needed groceries and other supplies, and she couldn't very well walk the fifteen miles to Glade Springs. Maybe she could hitch a ride into town with Aiden tonight. He could drop her off at the rental agency before picking up his date. But by the looks of things, he was about ready to go.

Summer headed for the door, tapping Patches on the head as she passed. "You stay here. I'll be back in a few minutes." She swung open the door and stopped short as she encountered a wall of red roses.

"I thought I'd apologize again for Zoe's behavior." The enormous bouquet of flowers lowered, revealing Dr. Devin Paxton's beseeching features. "And I thought maybe I could make it up to you over dinner."

No way. Although she'd considered the possibility that Aiden was right about what Devin would do, she hadn't really expected this. And certainly not so soon. They hadn't even reached the twenty-four-hour mark.

When she didn't speak, he added, "Or, we could take a walk later and enjoy the stars."

Summer had to bite her lip to keep from grinning. Aiden had nailed it. "I...don't know what to say."

"Say yes." He handed over the flowers.

She *could* say yes. Devin had a safe occupation. He seemed pleasant enough. But, Aiden had guessed Devin's actions so far, and if Aiden was right about the other things, the no-commitment attitude would be a deal breaker.

Summer wrapped her hands around the flower stems. "Actually, I was on my way out. My nephew is coming to live with me for a while, and I've got a ton of things to do to get ready."

Devin's brows drew together. "Your nephew? You knew I moved here to get away from kids." He rubbed his clean-shaven jaw. "Why didn't you tell me about him?"

Summer's defenses rose. "Zack is fifteen. He's not a kid."

Devin backed up a step. "How long will he be here?"

"He's staying until school starts in the fall."

"I see."

"What is it exactly that you see?" Summer stiffened.

"I uh…" Devin eased farther away. "Sounds like you'll be busy for a long time. I'd better get back to unpacking. Enjoy the flowers." He turned and disappeared into his apartment.

As his door closed, Aiden's door opened. Summer had no time to digest what had just transpired before Aiden's gaze zoned in on her first, and then the flowers. Crossing his arms, he sauntered across the hall. He hitched a chin toward the roses. "Was I right? An apology followed by a dinner invitation?"

"Yep." *And then a quick escape.*

"Figures." Aiden stepped beside her, leaned a shoulder on her doorframe, and crossed his ankles. If not for his twitching jaw muscle, she would guess he was completely at ease. "Did you accept?"

She didn't owe him an explanation, but for some reason she wanted to give him one. "He changed his mind when he found out my nephew, Zack, is coming to live with me for the remainder of the summer. Apparently the pediatrician doesn't want to spend his downtime around teenagers."

Aiden's disapproval of Devin showed through his tightening features. "So if not for Zack's visit, would you have agreed to go out with him?"

"Would it matter to you if I had?"

"Yes. Probably more than it should." Aiden's forthcoming admission made Summer's knees weak.

She should remind him they could only be friends, but conflicting emotions kept her from mentioning the *f* word. If not for Aiden's profession, she would be diving in head-first with him.

Aiden continued to wait for an answer. He

probably wouldn't budge from the doorway without one.

"No. I don't want to date him."

The creases between Aiden's brows eased and his lips curved into a smile. "Good." He relaxed his stance and looked at the roses. "May I take one?"

"Of course." She had plenty. Two dozen to be exact. But what was he going to do with it?

Aiden took up a rose and twirled it between fingers. "I'd better get going. I don't want to be late for my date."

What? Aiden was going to give *her* rose to *his* date? She stood stunned as he headed toward the stairs. Only he didn't go to the stairs. He walked to Dottie's apartment and knocked. What in the world?

Dottie opened her door and stepped out, wearing a shimmery dress and makeup.

Aiden leaned forward and presented the flower.

"How thoughtful of you." She accepted the rose.

Aiden bent his elbow and offered his arm. "Ready?"

"I'm always up for bingo." Dottie slipped her hand inside the crook of his elbow. Then, as if she'd just noticed Summer, she grinned from ear to ear. "I got the best out of all the bachelors at the auction."

Summer—relieved Dottie had claimed the winning prize—began to relax. "You sure did. But I thought bingo was on Friday nights. It's Wednesday."

"They're having an additional bingo night this week with extra-special prizes."

"Better than tickets to a bachelor auction?"

"I doubt that, but I'll find out." Dottie and Aiden moved toward the stairs.

"Wait." In all that had happened, she'd almost

forgotten why she'd left her apartment to begin with. "Can I come with you?"

Aiden's gaze jerked to hers, a smile playing on his lips. "You'll have to wait your turn. I'm a one woman kind of guy."

Yeah, she'd assumed so. To hear him say it made her ache for what she couldn't have. Or rather, wouldn't allow herself to have. "I need a ride into town to pick up a rental car. You can drop me off at the door and be on your way."

"In that case, I suppose I can make an exception."

15

Aiden had second thoughts the moment the first raindrops hit the windshield. He flipped on the wipers and glanced in the rearview mirror. Summer sat quietly in the backseat, looking out the window. If she noticed it was getting dark and a storm was ready to break loose, she didn't show it.

Dottie sat alongside him in the passenger seat, pleased as could be to have an official firefighter escorting her to bingo at the fire station. She chatted about a number of topics, but Aiden didn't keep up with everything she said as he concentrated on driving.

The stretch of road where Summer's accident had occurred came into view; the tire tracks were still visible. He slowed around the curve and glanced at Summer again. She'd gone pale, and the delicate pulse on her neck beat hard against her skin. She'd acted brave that night. As if she'd had a fender bender. But he knew better. Accidents like that had long-lasting effects.

The last thing he wanted was to drop her off at a car rental agency and leave her to find her way back through a storm so soon after the crash. "Why don't you stay with us tonight and play bingo? I've got the next few days off. I can bring you back tomorrow to pick up a car."

Summer's gaze shot up. "I...I couldn't impose. I'm sure you have other things to do. And, tonight is Dottie's night."

Dottie shifted around. "Impose? On what? Honey, if I was fifty years younger, I would've snatched Aiden off the market in a heartbeat." She gave an exaggerated wink. "But seeing as how this isn't a real date, I say the more the merrier."

"I have plenty of time to help you out," Aiden assured her. He'd spend every day with her if he could.

"I don't know. I should get back to Patches."

Dottie waved a hand. "He'll be fine. It's you I worry about. I just bring him over to keep you company."

Summer leaned forward. "All this time, Patches has been looking after me and not the other way around?"

"I thought you would've figured it out by now." Dottie twisted and reached between the front bucket seats to pat Summer's knee. "Don't you worry. You'll find a man sooner or later, then I'll get my dog back."

"You are rotten," Summer said, but through the rearview mirror, Aiden caught a glimpse of a smile.

He gripped the wheel and turned the wipers on high as heavy rain assaulted the windshield. No way would he turn her loose in these driving conditions, especially after seeing her reaction near the accident site. "What do you say? Will you come with us?"

"I suppose it would be all right."

Aiden let out a breath. "Good." Now he wouldn't have to drag her into the fire station against her wishes. It would've caused a scene, but he would've done it to keep her safe.

He drove past the rental agency and continued to the station. Cars overflowed from the parking lot and into the field next to the firehouse.

Aiden had volunteered to work bingo night multiple times, helping out with tasks ranging from selling concessions to calling out the numbers, and he'd seen turnouts like this before, but not very often.

He pulled into a parking spot reserved for firefighters and cut the engine. He met Summer's gaze through the rearview mirror. "I've got one umbrella. I'll walk Dottie in first and then come back for you."

Summer nodded. Her gaze darted from the three apparatus bays with their large opened doors, to the left side of the building housing the offices, training rooms, and residential areas. "I hadn't paid attention the night of the auction, but everything looks very well-kept."

Aiden appreciated that she'd noticed. He and the other firefighters took pride in keeping the station clean and well-maintained. "I'd be glad to show you around."

"I'd like that."

Maybe she'd gain a new perspective. He had a calling to be a firefighter. If they were to eventually have a romantic relationship, she'd have to accept his career and all that it entailed. Then again, she'd been upfront about her feelings. He had no right to want or expect anything else. But how could he temper the pull of attraction? He'd been drawn to her at first sight and when he'd extracted her from the wrecked car, an undeniable bond had formed.

Father, please give Summer the courage to work through her fears and accept me as I am—as You've created me to be.

A sense of peace settled over him, and he stepped into the pouring rain, opened the umbrella, and helped Dottie inside.

Dottie patted his hand. "Take your time showing Summer around. I'll get us a table." She melded into the crowd, greeting her friends as she selected a few items from the baked goods table.

Satisfied Dottie was otherwise engaged, Aiden made his way back to his truck. Summer climbed out and huddled underneath the umbrella alongside him. He took the opportunity to wrap an arm around her and tug her close. Warmth radiated beneath his palm and her sweet honeysuckle scent captivated him.

"Ready?" Summer looked into his eyes.

He'd never been so ready in his life. Oh, wait. She wasn't talking about dating. He gathered his wits and led the way. Once inside, he released her and folded the umbrella. Rain had splattered on his shoulders and pant legs. He plucked at the damp material, if for no other reason than to buy himself some time. The woman had a strong hold on him and probably didn't even know it. If she could get to him with a mere innocent touch, what would it be like if—

"So is this the room where you normally keep the fire engines?" Summer glanced around the large space, now occupied by bingo players, rectangular folding tables, and metal chairs.

Aiden brought his focus back to where it should be. "Yes. This is the apparatus bay." He gently touched his hand to the small of her back; he wasn't ready to relinquish physical contact. "Over there"—he pointed right—"is where we perform vehicle maintenance."

Summer nodded, taking it all in.

A glimmer of hope sprang to life. She didn't look as if she wanted to avoid all things having to do with firefighting. "Come on. I'll give you a tour." He led her past bingo players and through a set of doors. "This is the main entrance. We have training rooms to the left. The captain's office is over here." Aiden knocked on an open door and peeked in.

Captain Warren sat at his desk, filling out paperwork. He looked up, his gaze catching on Aiden and Summer. A smile caused creases near his eyes to deepen as he stood. "Summer Cassel, I presume?"

She nodded, stepped forward, and shook his hand. "How did you know?"

"Aiden talks about you all the time."

"Really?" Summer cast a curious glance toward Aiden. "Good things, I hope."

Aiden crossed his arms and shrugged with innocence. "I'll never tell."

She grinned. "Don't be too sure about that. I have my ways."

He caught the sparkle of humor in her gorgeous eyes. She could have her way with him, if she chose. But he kept that thought private.

Captain Warren eased back into his desk chair. "I'm glad to see you two finally got together."

Aiden cringed. Oh, boy. Guess he should've kept the captain better informed. "We're just friends. I'm showing her around the station."

"Friends?" Captain Warren shook his head. "Who are you trying to fool? I've seen newlyweds with less sparks than you two."

Summer's face turned the color of a ripe raspberry. Aiden wouldn't deny the attraction, but it looked as if she wanted to crawl under the desk and hide from it. She glanced everywhere but at him. "Is there…um…a ladies' room close by?"

"Across the hall. Second door on the right," Aiden instructed.

Summer nodded and scooted from the office.

"Was it something I said?" Captain Warren shuffled papers. "I thought you were going to ask her out?"

"I was." Aiden propped a hip on the desk's edge. "Then she found out I was a firefighter."

"And that's a problem because…?"

"Her sister was married to a police officer who lost his life in the line of duty, so Summer won't date anyone in a risky profession."

Captain Warren's gaze softened. "Then it looks like you have your work cut out for you."

"How so? She's made up her mind."

"I've never known you to back down from a challenge. Besides, you're half in love with her already. Given time, there will be no turning back."

16

Summer patted her face dry and looked in the mirror. The cold water had done nothing to erase the blush staining her cheeks.

Captain Warren—a sturdy man looking to be a handful of years older than Aiden—had called it as he'd seen it. There were sparks flying.

But even so, she couldn't allow them to ignite a fire that couldn't be contained.

Aiden deserved better.

How had she ended up in the fire station anyway? She should be stocking up on food for Zack. She should be cleaning her spare bedroom or paying bills. She should be anywhere but here, so why was she anxious to learn more about Aiden's day-to-day life?

Conflicting emotions ran a gamut. Round and round they went, making her head spin.

A knock sounded at the door. "You OK in there?"

Aiden would be wondering why she was taking so long. "I'll be out in a minute." Summer touched up her lipstick and checked her hair. The rain and heavy humidity had taken its toll, and she scrunched the top to give it a little volume before opening the door.

Aiden waited in the hallway, one foot propped against the white cinderblock wall and hands tucked into pockets. He didn't say anything as his gaze swept over her. Then again, he didn't have to say a word to take away her breath. This thing she had for him wasn't going away without a fight.

Summer cleared her throat. "So...what's next?"

He quirked a brow. "That's up to you."

"We can only be friends. Really. It's the only way."

An odd look crossed his features, and he ran a hand over his jaw. "I meant, what would you like to see next? The day room? Kitchen?"

"Oh." Summer spun the ring on her finger, willing herself not to blush all over again. But it didn't work. Heat climbed her cheeks. "Do you have a fitness room?"

"Absolutely." Aiden grinned and led Summer toward the back. "I spend quite a bit of time in there."

"It shows. You have a great...I mean...you're in good shape."

"Be careful. Keep up the compliments and you'll spoil me for other women."

"I'm sure I'm not the only woman to notice you're physically fit."

"It's usually the uniform that gets attention."

"You think so?"

"I know so." As they approached the fitness room, Aiden stopped at the glass door. "The last couple of women I went out with were more interested in what I represent than in who I am. They wanted a hero in their lives, and when they discovered I'm a real human being with both strengths and weaknesses, they lost interest."

"People can be shallow." Summer shrugged and then smiled. "At least you won't have to worry about that with me. I avoid dating uniformed men."

Aiden didn't return her smile—so much for trying to lighten the mood.

He moved in close, took her chin in hand, and tilted her face until their gazes met. His blue eyes held her transfixed. "I understand where you're coming from. You're scared. I get that. But I want you to know I plan on being around a long, long time. I spend a lot of time training and I take every precaution to remain as safe as possible."

He barely touched her, but he might as well have glued her to the spot. A delicious shiver skirted along her spine as he pleaded with his eyes. He wanted a chance with her. But could she risk her heart?

"Think about it." He released her chin and opened the door. As if the subject completely changed, he showed her around the fitness room. "We do a lot of strength training. Pull-ups, squats, sit-ups, that kind of thing."

Summer looked around, but the types of equipment didn't register. Her thoughts had ground to a halt with his quiet request. *Think about it.* She didn't want to think about it. She wanted to keep Aiden in the friendship category she'd placed him in. Why wasn't it working?

Oh, Lord. What am I going to do?

"Want to see the day room? We have theatre seats and a large-screen TV."

"Sure." Anything to get her mind off of how he could so easily affect her.

He led the way to a spacious room outfitted with several recliners and a TV that claimed a considerable portion of wall space.

"Do you ever get to watch movies here?" Maybe if she kept her mind on ordinary things, she could function normally.

"Sometimes, but it all depends on what calls come in. We start out the shift at eight in the morning. Take roll call and receive our assignments for the day. We routinely perform equipment checks, clean house, and exercise. We take turns doing the grocery shopping and cooking."

"Sounds like you live here."

"In a sense, I do." Aiden guided her into the kitchen.

A commercial-grade oven and stove and a set of deep sinks and stainless-steel appliances gave the room a high-quality look, while small touches of honey-colored accents warmed the atmosphere. "So, the people you work with…are you close to them?"

"They are as close to a family as I've ever known."

Summer remembered he'd said he'd grown up in an orphanage. Her heart squeezed tight. She'd been raised in a loving home. Her parents worked long hours, and she'd often resented the fact they were away so much, but at least they had been there to tuck her in at night. "Is that why you chose to be a firefighter? To have a family?"

Aiden withdrew two bottles of water from the fridge and offered her one. "It's not why I signed up, but it's a great benefit."

Summer accepted the bottle and sat at the long rectangular table. "Have you always known what you wanted to do?"

"Since I was eight." Aiden took a seat opposite her. "The fire department came to Hope Haven to give the kids a chance to climb on fire engines, try on helmets, and learn about fire safety."

"We had firefighters come to my school every year. It was a lot of fun."

"Well, I had fun too. But it was more than that for me. God put it on my heart that day to be a firefighter. I knew that's what I was destined to do. As I grew older, I saw it as a way to give back to the community that helped raise me. I don't know where I would've ended up if not for the generosity of others."

"I didn't realize there were traditional types of orphanages anymore."

"Hope Haven isn't exactly traditional. It's a community made up of a group of foster homes in a central location. Usually, eight to ten kids live in each house, with a community center nearby where the kids gather for recreation, special events, and holiday meals. I met a lot of great people there."

"Now that you're a firefighter, do you go back and visit the kids? Show them your fire engine and let them wear your helmet?"

"Every so often we take out the ladder truck. The kids love it," Aiden confirmed with a smile that brightened his eyes.

Summer understood his exuberance; she felt the same way about her career. She couldn't begrudge Aiden for finding his niche, but she still wished what he did for a living wasn't so dangerous.

She glanced around the kitchen. "Do you cook too?"

"Sure do." He took a sip of water. "Chicken potpie is my specialty."

"You are getting harder and harder to resist."

"Is that so?" He leaned forward. "I guess I should add that I do dishes, too. And I clean."

"Clean? As in dust? Mop? Sanitize toilet bowls?"

"Yep. Till they shine."

"Oh, my." Summer plastered a hand to her heart. "What more could a woman ask for?"

Aiden's smile slowly faded. He dipped his head, fiddled with the wrapper on his water bottle. He caught an edge and peeled the thin plastic away before meeting her gaze again. "I guess the risky job cancels out all the good stuff, huh?"

"I…" Summer's lungs constricted. What could she say? And why did she keep getting herself into these sticky situations? "I don't want to hurt you."

"And you don't want to be hurt. I know. But aren't some things worth the risk?"

Anxiety struck at the mere thought. She pictured Riley, devastated. Zack, without a father. Fear closed her throat. How could she willingly put herself in that position?

A group of firefighters strode into the kitchen.

The tension in the room dissolved as Aiden nodded at the crowd. "Joe, William, Marilyn. This is Summer." Aiden stood as he introduced them. "She's my…" He met her gaze as she sat rooted to the hard wooden chair. "Neighbor."

True. They were neighbors. So why did his answer sting? She wouldn't have minded if he'd used the *f* word this time. Summer pushed past the disappointment and smiled as Aiden's coworkers greeted her with handshakes.

"Thought you were off tonight?" Marilyn, a tall, dark-haired woman, commented as she headed to the fridge.

"We came to play bingo." Aiden stepped around the table. "Speaking of which, we'd better get going. I've left my date alone for too long."

His comment startled Summer, then it registered. Dottie. She'd forgotten the entire reason they were there.

By time they made it back to the main area, Dottie had spread out her bingo cards and arranged ink daubers in neat lines. She'd also surrounded the entire area with 1980s troll dolls.

"For good luck," Dottie explained when Summer gave her a questioning look. "Although really, luck has nothing to do with it. God gives me all my blessings."

"I haven't seen these in years." She sat beside Dottie, while Aiden settled across the table facing them. Summer picked up a doll that wore a fire chief's hat and firefighter gear. "Have you had this all this time? Or did you find it secondhand somewhere?"

"I bought him when he was brand new. He started the tradition. These guys have been playing with me for decades. I think that's why I won the ticket to the bachelor auction." She patted the little fireman doll on his fluffy head, leaned close to its ear, and whispered, "Now, you can help me win that basket of embroidery items. Or the gift certificates for the whitewater-rafting trip."

Aiden shared a smile with Summer. "I'll go get us some cards."

"OK. But I don't expect to win." She lifted a cute little troll dressed in purple, reminiscing. "When I was little, my sister gave me her entire collection of Pound Puppies. I should've kept them for days like today."

"No need for vintage toys. I'll be your real-life collectible. From God," Aiden offered with a wink as he strolled away.

Dottie pretended like she hadn't heard. But Summer knew better. The woman's smile gave her away.

17

Summer parked the compact rental car and unloaded tons of groceries. Her stomach had dropped at the price she'd paid, but she didn't know what Zack would like, so she'd bought a variety of foods. She filled her pantry with items she hadn't bought in years. She shoved boxes of vanilla and chocolate snack cakes beside her long-grain brown rice, telling herself a few treats wouldn't hurt a growing teenager.

A container of orange juice went into the fridge. She folded an empty plastic grocery bag and stuffed it in the recycle bin, hoping the performance of everyday tasks would keep her from thinking of Aiden. As of yet, the plan hadn't worked. He crept into her mind no matter what she was doing.

When Aiden had dropped her off at the rental car agency earlier, he had offered to follow her to the grocery store and help her with menu planning. He seemed to want to be around her no matter what she was doing, even routine things. She'd never had a man grocery shop with her before. Then again, she'd never had a guy offer to be only friends before either.

She'd had boyfriends over the years and had even made a stab at a semi-serious relationship once, but overall, her main focus had been her career. Meeting Aiden had opened her mind to other possibilities. But there had to be an assortment of single men in safe occupations within a reasonable radius of Glade Springs.

Take Dr. Paxton, for example. Other than his obvious aversion to children, he seemed like a decent guy, and she knew plenty of women who would love to date someone like him.

So why wasn't she interested in the slightest?

Aiden had some kind of hold on her. That's why. What if Aiden was part of God's plan for her life and she pushed him away out of fear? *Lord, You know what's in my heart. Am I wrong to want to protect myself from being hurt? From losing someone I could possibly love?* As she continued to pray, Summer finished storing the groceries and headed to the spare bedroom. She rearranged boxes she hadn't touched since moving in, stuffing a few in the closet and squeezing some in a corner to make the space functional.

Maybe Zack could bring posters with him to hang on the wall or a put up a corkboard and fill it with pictures. Did teenagers still do those things? Or had the world evolved since she'd been that age? What if she had no way to relate to Zack now that he was older? Perhaps she'd try the ice cream route after all. A double-dipped cone of dark chocolate had yet to let her down.

The thought of dessert reminded her about the blackberry cobbler she had spilled on Aiden. She had time on her hands. She could make a trip to the blackberry brambles and prepare another cobbler for him. The idea had her pulse spiking. The last visit to the river hadn't turned out as she'd planned, but she had to get back out there sometime. Today was as good a day as any.

But before she went to all the effort, she'd better be certain Aiden would be home tonight. She exited her apartment and crossed the hallway, knocked twice, and waited.

A moment later, Aiden opened his door. "Hey. Everything OK?" He was fully dressed and held keys in his hands.

"Are you headed out? I can come back later."

"Actually, I am. There's a fire in an abandoned building on the edge of town. It's close to a residential neighborhood, so Captain Warren called me in for backup. We've got to get it under control before it spreads to nearby homes." He stepped out, locked his door.

Summer tamped sudden unease. Aiden was highly trained. Fighting fires was his job. But would she ever get used to the idea? "I won't keep you any longer then. If you want to come by when you get home, I'll have another blackberry cobbler ready and waiting."

"Sounds good." Aiden gave an appreciative smile. "I'll be looking forward to it."

As soon as Aiden drove away, Summer wasted no time in digging out the kayak, paddling upriver to the brambles, and selecting the juiciest blackberries. The birds had found her stash, so finding enough took a little longer than the first time. Even so, she managed to harvest what she needed and made it back to The Meadows without incident.

Within twenty minutes, the fresh, soothing scents of melted butter and warm fruit drifted from the oven. She glanced out the window, looking for Aiden's truck. No signs of it yet. By the time she took out the cobbler and set it on the stovetop to cool, she'd checked half a dozen times to see if he'd returned. The sun had set, and she couldn't shake the feeling something had gone wrong.

Summer plopped onto the couch and flipped open a magazine. She turned the pages, not really seeing anything. "He's fine. He's doing his job." Hearing the words spoken aloud didn't convince her. A niggling sensation took hold and wouldn't let go. If her worry and anxiety was this bad when they were only friends, how much worse would it be if they were a couple? Would she spend every evening they were apart pacing floors? If she could only have enough faith to drive out the worry crowding her mind...

Summer picked up her daily devotional and found one of her favorite Scriptures ready and waiting. *"For I know the plans I have for you," declares the Lord, "plans to prosper you and not to harm you, plans to give you hope and a future."*

She closed her eyes and prayed, "Lord, please protect Aiden and the other firefighters, and forgive me for worrying. I know I should rely on You and have faith that everything will work out for the good of Your kingdom."

Summer sat quietly for a few minutes, until she couldn't stay still any longer. She shoved to her feet and checked the parking lot one more time. No Aiden.

She turned on the TV, hoping to distract herself, but froze when a breaking news story came on—a petite, blonde reporter stood in front of a raging fire as it consumed a two-story home.

"Tragedy has struck the Gibson family in Glade Springs. Their house caught fire tonight when sparks from a fire in an abandoned warehouse reached their property. Three people were inside the house at the time. Mr. and Mrs. Gibson have since been rescued, but they are frantic as their seven-year-old son is still inside."

Summer's heart skipped and her stomach dropped. She cranked up the volume as if she could pull more information through the speakers.

"Two firefighters from Glade Springs Volunteer Fire Department remain in the home, but no one else can get in as conditions deteriorate. Just one moment." The reporter placed a hand on her ear as if listening through an earpiece. "Apparently, communication has been compromised. Firefighters Marilyn Ellis and Aiden Hawk are now on their own."

"Aiden..." Summer sprang to her feet so fast a wave of dizziness ensued. *Lord, get them out.*

The house had become a deathtrap. Flames gushed from windows and doors. Smoke clogged the sky. How could anyone still be alive inside? Excruciating moments passed as the camera focused on the inferno. Then finally, a firefighter stumbled out the door, followed by another carrying a child. All three people were covered in soot and ash.

The first one out removed her face mask, and Summer recognized Marilyn from when they'd met at the firehouse. The other firefighter strode toward the waiting ambulance, handed over the child's limp form. Then, he removed his mask.

Relief flooded through Summer upon seeing Aiden's face. But the relief was momentary; Aiden's features showed grave concern as he kept his focus on the boy. "He's not responding." The reporter's microphone caught Aiden's words to the EMTs.

The boy's parents gathered around, and soon they all jammed into the ambulance. Sirens exploded as they headed toward the hospital, leaving Aiden looking after them. The camera zoomed in on Aiden's taut features before he turned and disappeared from view.

"That was a close call..." The reporter began talking again.

Summer turned off the television and sat in the quiet stillness.

If Aiden was hers, how would she cope with nights like tonight? *It's not about you.* The soft words spoken to her heart jolted her to her core. What must things be like for him? How could *he* cope?

Aiden displayed confidence and self-assurance when it came to his career. Rescuing people was his life. His chosen profession. But the image flashed in her mind of his drawn features as he looked over the unconscious child. He'd be devastated if the boy didn't live.

He needs you. There it was again; the small, still voice.

Summer knew what she had to do. She couldn't control the boy's fate, but she could comfort Aiden when he returned home. She stepped onto the balcony and looked into the darkness. She'd wait as long as necessary, fully aware this night might prove to be one of the longest of her life.

18

Aiden exited the fire station at midnight. He'd showered and was clean on the outside, but a mess on the inside. He'd signed up for this sort of thing, he reminded himself. But it wasn't every day a child's life hung in the balance. In spite of efforts from multiple crews, the house had been on fire for several minutes when he had arrived. He'd done everything he could to get Kyle Gibson out before it was too late. But had his efforts been enough?

Marilyn had similar concerns, but she'd reminded him before heading home that Kyle had a family to stand by his side. And she had a family to grasp onto as well. She had a husband and two children of her own.

Aiden's desire to have his own family expanded to an all-time high. Summer came to mind. She had invited him for cobbler, but she'd surely be asleep by now, which left him with an empty apartment to go home to. Not exactly what he'd prefer, given the choice.

Resigned to a sleepless night ahead, he kept his radio off as he drove home, his mind playing over the images of the limp boy he'd carried out. Although the fire hadn't reached the child's bedroom, the smoke inhalation could prove to be deadly. *Father, let him be OK.*

Assured God had heard his prayer and had the situation under His control, Aiden turned onto the tree-lined drive and eased his truck along the gravel road. As he rounded toward The Meadows and approached the parking lot, his gaze strayed to Summer's apartment.

A light shone through her windows and the French doors stood open.

His heart jolted. She normally turned out her lights by ten or eleven. Had something happened while he was gone? He parked and jogged to the wraparound porch, darted into the foyer, and took the steps two at a time.

Summer stood waiting in the hallway as if she'd seen him drive in. Her brows were pinched together and she was wringing her hands, but she looked unharmed. She wore a pair of navy sweatpants, a white tank top, and had her hair pulled into a ponytail. She looked young, innocent, and concerned.

He stepped close. "I thought you'd be asleep by now."

"I saw the news." Her voice shook.

A mixture of emotions cascaded through him. Had she waited up for him?

She tucked her lower lip between her teeth as if hesitant as to what to say next. After a moment, she stepped forward and wrapped her arms around his waist, pressing tight against him.

The compassionate gesture reached his soul. He folded her into his arms, rested his cheek on the top of her head, and inhaled her sweet honeysuckle scent. Heartbeats collided. Warmth seeped through clothes. She had waited. He wasn't alone. No more pretending. "I don't think this friendship thing is going to work out for us."

She released her hold and slowly brought up her

wide-eyed gaze.

Cupping her face in his hands, Aiden smoothed his thumbs along her soft skin. "You are difficult to resist, Summer Cassel. Much more so than I could've imagined."

The pulse point at the base of her throat went wild. His heart rate matched hers. And although he'd promised himself he wouldn't cross the line—he bent his head and kissed her.

She sucked in a breath. And why wouldn't she be surprised?

They'd agreed to only be friends.

But he tested those boundaries, coaxing a response until she finally relaxed and slid her lips against his. He lost himself in the moment. Every emotion poured out, melding with hers. When he eased away, he met her dazed eyes. "You feel it too, don't you?" He didn't need to explain what the 'it' was. If she felt the same, she'd know.

She merely nodded and his hopes soared. She *had* felt the searing connection.

Encouraged, he steadied his gaze on hers. "I think we should give this a shot. You and me."

She blinked and then retreated from his grasp. "I need time. I...I wasn't expecting this."

"I wasn't either." How had things progressed so rapidly? Only a short time ago, he was afraid to talk to her. Then he'd gotten past that and they'd tried the friendship route, for all the good that had done. That hadn't even lasted a week.

"I'm scared." Her whisper triggered his protective streak.

"I can't tell you what you want to hear. I can't promise I will come home safe each night. But I can assure you that I have one heart and it's intended for one woman."

"And you think that woman could be me?"

Perhaps it was too soon to tell. But from everything he'd experienced so far, Summer could be an answer to his prayers.

He replied with a slow grin. "There's only one way to find out."

~*~

Aiden had made his position clear. He wanted more than friendship. No more subtle hints. No more harmless flirting. Summer appreciated his direct approach. And his kiss...well, that had blown her away. She had sensed the strength of his conviction through his touch. But a faint scent of smoke still clung to him, reminding her of where he'd come from. What he'd done. And the dangers involved.

She couldn't simply bow to her emotions. That would leave her exposed to potential heartbreak. But how could she deny him without consideration? Something unspoken had passed between them, something bigger than attraction, deeper than friendship. Something she couldn't name, or ignore.

"I could go for something warm and sweet right now." Aiden glanced toward Summer's door. "If it's not too late, is your offer still open?"

"O-offer?" Summer stumbled on the word. His unexpected kiss had been warm and sweet. Her lips still tingled and her entire being endured aftershocks.

"You said you were going to make a cobbler?"

"Oh. Right. Yes. I did." Reining in fanciful thoughts, she nodded, turned, and led the way into her apartment, all the while willing her heart to stop beating out of her chest.

Summer stepped into the living room and a breeze caught her by surprise. She'd left the doors open to the balcony and humid air warmed the room. "I must've forgotten to shut—"

A deep purring sound came from her kitchen. Summer stopped mid-step and whirled around. Tom cat lounged on her countertop, hunching over the cobbler. He glanced up. Stained whiskers held evidence of his eating binge as he licked guilty lips.

"No. You. Did. Not," Summer gasped.

Oh, but I did, Tom's green eyes mocked.

Summer lunged.

Tom sprang into action. His hind legs kicked the cobbler's remains as he scrambled for freedom. The pan flew through the air. Summer's stomach dropped as her second attempt at a cobbler met its untimely demise. Blackberries turned to mush and golden-brown crust smeared across the tiled kitchen floor.

At least the stain-bearing fruit hadn't landed on Aiden this time. He stayed in the background, his gaze taking it all in.

Tom managed to escape, and the room fell silent.

Aiden's lips twitched and then he smoothed a hand over his mouth as if to conceal his grin.

"You think this is funny?" Summer posted hands on hips.

"No," he said, but his shoulders shook a couple of times.

Oh, well. Better to laugh than to cry. Summer chuckled once, and then fell into a fit of uncontrollable giggles as she allowed herself the much-needed release.

Aiden joined her uninhibited laughter, and before long, his features showed no traces of strain. "Guess I'll have to wait longer for my housewarming gift." Aiden sobered and strolled to the kitchen, gathered paper towels, and began wiping up the mess.

Summer closed the doors and joined Aiden. "I'm not sure I should bother making another one. Seems like I'm wasting my time."

"Believe me. You're not." His gaze seared into hers and his sincere, low voice held vulnerability. "It's especially difficult to go home to an empty apartment on nights like tonight. Cobbler or no cobbler, I appreciate your efforts. And your company."

After seeing the news broadcast, not waiting had never been an option. "Do you know if the boy you rescued will be OK?"

Aiden finished wiping the floor and settled onto a barstool. "Not yet. Captain Warren said he'd give me a call when he found out."

Summer grabbed a mop and rinsed off the cobbler's sticky remains as she imagined what Aiden must feel. "It has to be difficult. Waiting. Not knowing."

"It is. Was it hard for you, too? Waiting for me?"

She wouldn't deny it. "Yes. I don't know how many nights I could do this without losing my mind." Even though Tom cat had created a much-needed distraction, the emotional evening had taken its toll.

"You're stronger than you give yourself credit for. You survived the river. The car accident."

True. But could she survive loving a man like Aiden Hawk?

19

Witnessing Aiden's heroic efforts and then his vulnerability had touched Summer on a primal level—he'd made an impression that would be imprinted on her heart forever. What she would ultimately choose to do with that deepening bond, she hadn't a clue. For now, she had other pressing matters to focus on. Saturday had rolled around.

Zack would be here any minute, and Summer's stomach knotted into a complex array of tangles. At fifteen, Zack was old enough to come and go as he wished, within limits. She wanted to know where he was going, who he planned to be with, and she wanted him home by ten o'clock each night. Figuring out how to enforce her rules would be tricky. She'd always been his fun-loving aunt who got away with giving him lollipops before dinner and spoiling him with shopping trips to the toy store. But those days were over. *Lord, help me know how to relate to him.*

A knock on the door had her jumping up and swinging the door open wide. She'd expected to see Riley and Zack. Possibly Aiden or Dottie. But instead, Dr. Devin Paxton stood in front of her with arms full of moving boxes and a humble smile.

"I wanted to apologize about the other day. How I ran off so fast. I didn't mean to be rude."

It was kind of strange how he'd reacted to the news of Zack coming to visit, but she hadn't thought much about it since. She eyed the boxes. "Getting settled in OK?"

"I've got a ways to go, but it's coming along. I'm afraid I picked up too many boxes at once. My mother would write me out of her will if I broke any pieces of her china." The boxes teetered and he worked to balance them. "My door's shut. Would you mind?"

"Of course." Summer scooted past him. She stepped across the hall and opened his door.

"Mom's loaning these to me, hoping I'll throw a dinner party for her and my dad's fortieth anniversary." Devin kept talking as he set down the boxes in the kitchen.

Summer lingered in the doorway. "Forty years. That's wonderful."

"It's a miracle if you ask me." He dusted his hands and returned to the foyer. "Dad's an orthopedic surgeon. Mom's an editor for a fashion magazine. They couldn't be more different. But somehow, they make it work." He waved her inside. "Come on in."

"Where's Zoe?" Summer searched the floor for the Chihuahua.

"Don't worry. She's safely tucked away in a kennel. I didn't want her getting out as I'm moving in things."

Summer eased into the living room. The space looked fully furnished, with modern art pieces decorating the walls. Everything in the room was either black or white. The museum-quality décor looked sterile. "No wonder you don't want kids in here. Your things look...expensive." She was surprised he had a dog. Might get fur on something.

"Apparently, I've given you the wrong impression. I love kids. I really do." Devin ducked his head as if imploring her to believe him.

"But you don't want them in your personal life." The room she stood in proved it. Everything screamed look but don't touch. She'd yet to see the inside of Aiden's apartment, but she'd bet it was decorated nothing like this.

"I might want kids one day. My mother is desperate for grandchildren. If she saw you, she'd have the two of us married and flying off to Europe in their private jet for a month-long honeymoon."

Chills wracked Summer's spine. She'd rather have a lifetime of root canals than be pressed into a mold of someone's idea of a perfect wife. She could be wrong, but she sensed any woman Devin was with would be held to impossibly high standards.

"Can I offer you something?" Devin rubbed his hands together. "An afternoon cocktail?"

"No, thanks. I don't drink."

"Oh." He scratched his head. "I have canned soda."

"I'm fine, really. I should get going. My sister and nephew will be arriving soon." She turned to leave. The door had swung shut behind her, and she hadn't even noticed.

Devin stepped in front of her. "I need to make a few more trips to the car. Would you mind holding the door open for me a couple of minutes?"

While not quite as tall as Aiden, Devin still had a good couple of inches on her. She didn't exactly feel intimidated, more like cornered. "I suppose I can spare a few minutes."

"Thanks." He opened the door and stepped forward. "Hey. How's it going?" Devin nodded to someone in the hallway.

Summer scooted around the door, expecting to

find Riley and Zack.

Instead, Aiden was walking past. His blue eyes widened and he stopped mid-step, his focus flicking toward Summer and the apartment she still stood inside.

Devin continued on his way downstairs, whistling a quiet tune as if oblivious to Aiden's reaction.

Dressed in swim trunks and a fire department T-shirt, with the scent of coconut sunscreen radiating around him, Aiden appeared ready to head out on the water. Instead, he spun on his heel and in three long strides reached her side. "Everything OK?"

"Yes. Sure. Why?" If he wanted to know why she was inside Devin's apartment, he'd have to ask.

He placed a hand on the doorframe, leaned in. "You know why." His words, like silk caressing her skin, slid over her.

Yes, she knew why. Aiden had appointed himself her protector. "Maybe I do. But I want to hear you say it."

"There are more ways than one to communicate." He wrapped an arm around her waist and lifted her against his solid, muscled chest as he backed her out of Devin's apartment. He set her down and then planted a kiss on her lips so passionate the world around her disappeared.

Everything faded—all her worries, fears, and doubts. Time ceased to exist. For the moment, Aiden was all that mattered.

"Whoa. I thought you two were just friends." Devin's voice broke through.

"Aunt Summer?" Another, younger male voice crept in.

A gasp sounded as a third person intruded on

their moment. Apparently, they'd gathered quite the audience.

Aiden released her.

Summer peeled open her eyes.

Three people stared back: Devin, Riley, Zack. Devin's brows drew together as if he were truly confused. Riley sported a smile. Zack shook his head, making his too-long brown hair shift over an eye.

"I want to go home." Zack broke the awkward silence.

Summer sent a helpless look toward Riley.

Riley shrugged. "Welcome to my world."

20

Aiden had gotten his point across. Too bad it had ended like this—a cherry-red blush bloomed on Summer's face as she stood speechless in front of her sister, nephew, and the scheming doctor.

Aiden had suspected Paxton hadn't given up, and he didn't trust the man past the plastic smile on his face—at least the guy wasn't smiling anymore.

Considering Summer's deer-in-the-headlights look, Aiden stepped forward and introduced himself to the petite red-headed woman in the navy pantsuit. Her facial features held some resemblance to Summer's, but that's where the commonalities ended. "Riley, I presume? I'm Aiden. Summer's friend and neighbor."

At several inches shorter than Summer, Riley had to crane her neck to look up at him. "Pleased to meet you."

"And you must be Zack." Aiden offered his hand to the teenager.

As if he would rather touch a poisonous snake, Zack narrowed his eyes.

"Be polite," his mother warned.

Zack tugged off the hood from his gray sweat jacket and reluctantly shook Aiden's hand, all the while eyeing him skeptically. He hiked up oversized jeans as he looked toward his mom. "Can I go now?"

"Go where?" Riley lifted manicured hands. "We just got here."

Summer blinked and straightened the hem of her

blouse. "Um...Riley, Zack, this is Dr. Paxton. He's one of my other neighbors. I was just holding the door open for him as he moves in."

So, the doctor needed help keeping a door open? Aiden could fix that. He excused himself long enough to grab a wedge of wood from his apartment. When he returned, he placed it under Devin's door, effectively keeping the entranceway free and clear. "This should take care of your problem." Aiden shot a pointed look at Paxton. "How about I give you a hand with the rest of your things?"

"Uh...OK. Thanks." Paxton nodded and scooted past them all to take an armful of boxes inside his apartment.

"I'm guessing the three of you have some catching up to do." Aiden touched Summer's elbow and placed a quick kiss on her cheek. "I'll see you later?" He held her gaze until she nodded.

Summer led Riley toward her apartment.

Aiden grabbed a couple of boxes from Paxton's car before returning upstairs. He ran into Zack lingering in the hallway. "Give it a few days. You might find that you like it here," Aiden suggested as he set the items in Paxton's foyer.

Zack approached the door. "What would you know about what I like?"

Ah. More than two words. There was hope. "I wouldn't. I'm just saying I grew up around here. There are lots of things for a guy your age to do."

"Like what? Counting cows?"

Aiden had met more than one skeptic in his day. "That would be boring. Cow tipping? Now, that's a thrill."

"You do that?"

"Used to."

"But isn't cow tipping illegal?"

"Well…that depends on whose cow you're messing with."

"I obviously don't own a cow, so are you suggesting I do something illegal?"

Aiden shook his head and hid a smile. This kid wouldn't make things easy, but he looked forward to the challenge. "How about we change subjects? You can give me a hand with Dr. Paxton's belongings."

Surprisingly enough, Zack fell into step beside him. "Why are you helping him? He's after your girl."

Aiden took the stairs slower than normal to buy more time with Zack. "Summer can make up her own mind about what she wants."

"Uh-huh. Looks like she was pretty cozy with you."

Aiden agreed. She'd kissed him back wholeheartedly. He didn't mind so much that Paxton witnessed the embrace. But he still wasn't so sure what Zack thought about it. "No need to worry. I have good intentions."

Zack scoffed. "You really are from around here, aren't you? Ever been to a real city?"

Aiden hid another smile as he opened the doors leading to the front porch. He allowed Zack to exit first.

Although a few passing clouds muted the sun's direct rays, humidity hung heavy and thick in the air, making it plenty warm enough for a kayak trip. But breaking the ice with Zack was much more important. This wasn't the first time Aiden had changed his plans on a moment's notice, and it wouldn't be the last. "I grew up here and attended the University of Virginia, but then I spent some time in Chicago. I worked a couple of years there and then moved back. I've been working at Glade Springs Volunteer Fire Department ever since. I'm one of a few paid professional fighters on the team."

"Geez. TMI, dude. It's not like I asked for your résumé."

Aiden chuckled under his breath. "We'll be spending some time around each other. Doesn't hurt to know a little about your neighbors."

"So, that's why you're helping Dr. Paxton," Zack muttered as they approached the convertible. "You're keeping watch over your enemy to make sure he doesn't steal Aunt Summer away with his flashy smile and big wallet."

The kid had an edge to him, no doubt about it. "It's not like that. Besides, around here no one takes what someone else isn't willing to give."

Zack smirked. "We'll see about that." He lifted a box from the car and headed inside.

Paxton jogged out and around to the trunk. "How'd you get him to help? A minute ago, it looked as if he wanted to take a swing at you for groping his aunt."

"I wasn't groping," Aiden defended, tempted to abandon his efforts at being civil.

Paxton picked up some items and stepped close, clapping Aiden on the shoulder. "No worries, man. You got to her first. I won't interfere."

As if the guy had a chance with her to begin with. Then again, Aiden wasn't positive yet that he even had a chance. With the last of the boxes in hand, Aiden followed Paxton upstairs, unsure where he fit in with Summer and her family, if he fit in at all.

21

As soon as Summer shut the door behind her, Riley turned with mouth agape. "Who is this Aiden Hawk guy, and where can I get one?"

Summer hid her shock at Riley's response. Since Doug's passing, Riley hadn't shown any interest in men whatsoever. "I told you before; he's my neighbor. You can't get one. He's one of a kind."

Riley plunked herself onto Summer's couch. "Why didn't you tell me he's so hot?"

"Because we're always talking about other things. Like how Zack is doing. Where is he anyway?"

"Probably exploring." Riley waved a hand.

"And I don't need to worry about that?"

"You'll get used to it." Riley pressed fingers to her temples, gently rubbing. "I hardly see him anymore."

Summer doubted she'd get used to being responsible for someone she couldn't keep in close range. The experience would be entirely new. At school, she had the kids contained in a classroom or a specialized occupational therapy room. "What should I do to keep him entertained? I want him to like it here."

"Don't worry too much about it. He'll probably resist anything you try. Just give him a few days to get settled. He might ask you to show him around Glade Springs. But I wouldn't count on it."

"Things will somehow work out." She hoped.

"I don't know what I'd do without you." Moisture gathered in Riley's eyes.

"And I don't know how you're managing without Doug," Summer countered. "You're a great mom. I hope you know that."

"You might not think that if you knew some of the things I've said to Zack. He makes me so angry sometimes. I just lose it." She leaned forward and smoothed a few strands of hair from her face. "That's part of the reason I decided to bring him here."

"How did you get him to agree to come?"

"I didn't give him much of a choice. I got a phone call from Doug's old partner a few days ago."

"Zack's in trouble again?" Summer's throat dried.

"It's worse than that. Leonard is moving to Detroit. He can't protect Zack anymore. Moving in with you very well may be Zack's last chance to stay out of jail. It's certainly the best opportunity for me to get him away from his so-called friends."

"These friends of his won't try to come here to see him." Summer's palms dampened. "Will they?"

"I doubt it. They don't have cars or the money to get a bus ticket. I'm just hoping he'll make some good friends here like he used to have. The kind with morals and decent values."

"I pray you're right. For now, let's get you settled. I have the one spare twin bed for Zack, and if you don't mind sleeping on the couch—"

"Actually, I hadn't planned on staying. I was afraid if I did, I'd change my mind. So I'll head back, find a motel somewhere."

"Are you sure?" Summer's pulse rate spiked. She wanted to scream for her sister not to leave her alone with Zack so soon, but she held her tongue. She had volunteered for this, after all.

"I'm positive. I'm desperate for a little me-time."

Everything in Riley's body language confirmed her words. Her eyes showed fatigue through red-rimmed lids, and dark circles curved underneath. "I'll be sure to keep close contact with you. And call me any time day or night if something happens."

Summer stood, paced the room. She needed air. "We should get his suitcases."

"He's only got one. He tends to wear the same clothes over and over." Riley stood and withdrew keys from her pocket. "I can hardly get him to take that zippered hoodie off."

"Seems like he'd get hot in it."

"You'd think." Riley shrugged. "But it's not a battle I'm willing to wage a war over."

"I understand that. I'll go get the suitcase," Summer offered, accepted the keys, and slipped into the hallway.

Devin's door stood open and Zack wandered out from inside the apartment.

"There you are." Summer stopped to greet him. "I thought maybe tomorrow you'd like to take out a kayak? Explore the river a little."

"Whatever." Zack stuffed fisted hands into his hoodie's pockets, rushed past her, and disappeared inside her apartment.

Well, so much for getting off to a good start. Summer felt a gray hair forming already. *Lord, what have I gotten myself into?*

22

Summer set up her lounge chair close to the river as she kept an eye on Zack. He paddled along the shoreline, choosing to float downriver even though she'd suggested he fight the current first and then drift back to The Meadows. She recalled her ordeal when Aiden had come to her rescue, and she fought sudden panic that Zack might not make it back, but the river flowed at normal water levels today, and no storms were forecasted. She had no reason to worry. And although she hoped Zack would keep the kayak within eyesight, she couldn't very well give him restrictive boundaries to relieve her unwarranted anxiety.

She settled into the chair, thankful for the towering oak near the river's edge, which cast shadows and protected her from the midday sun. She opened a romance novel, but couldn't concentrate on the words. She hadn't slept well last night. Everything from Zack's arrival to Riley's quick departure and Aiden's renewed show of determination spun in her mind. The complex web of emotions had left her more confused today than ever before.

"I hope I'm not interrupting."

Summer warmed at the sound of Aiden's voice. "Not at all."

He stood a few feet away, hands tucked into pockets. He looked humble, strong, and vibrant.

"I'm getting my feet wet with this temporary guardian thing. I could use a distraction from worrying about Zack paddling out of sight."

"You're doing a great job with him."

It hadn't even been a full day, so she didn't know how Aiden could think that, but she appreciated the encouragement. She scanned his beige swim trunks, white sleeveless T-shirt, and water shoes. "Going kayaking?"

"I was thinking about it."

OK. But he wasn't moving. He gazed at the river as if not really seeing it.

Summer set down the paperback. "Is there something on your mind?"

"Actually, there is." Aiden eased onto the ground beside her, propping elbows on his bent knees. "About yesterday." He plucked a blade of grass from a tall patch and spun it between fingers. "I'm afraid I might have come off a little stronger than I intended."

Summer straightened. "I don't regret the kiss. Do you?"

"Not in the way you might think. It's just…showing you how I feel is one thing. Pressuring you to feel the same way is something else entirely."

"I'm glad you understand. I have been thinking a lot about us. I mean what's happening between us."

A slight smile curved his lips. "I like the way 'us' sounds."

She did too, in spite of her reservations, and a shot of adrenaline spiked through her veins. She glanced away. The swirling current created a small whirlpool near the dock and a bright-green leaf spun in circles until it bumped the piling and made good its escape. "Every time I come out here, I notice something different. The river is always changing. Evolving in some way."

Aiden scooted a little closer. Close enough to touch her if he wanted. "Even if we try to resist change, it's inevitable."

Summer met Aiden's deep blue gaze. "I'm not against trying something new. I'm just leery of the unknown."

"I think most people feel that way at some point or another. But, that's where faith comes in."

They sat quietly for a few minutes. Summer relaxed against the folding lounge chair and tucked her legs under her. "I like spending time with you. I just hope I don't make a mess of things."

"You're kidding, right? Have you forgotten how I avoided you at all costs because I was too nervous to speak to you?"

"Saving my life more than makes up for our awkward beginning. Speaking of saving people, I heard on the news this morning that Kyle Gibson will be all right."

Aiden nodded. "Captain Warren called and let me know Kyle's expected to make a full recovery. I meant to tell you. That's why I originally came out here. That, and to apologize for pressuring you into a decision you're clearly not ready to make."

Maybe not, but in the span of a few short days, he'd broken more protective walls than any amount of therapy could ever have done. If she wasn't careful, she could fall in love with Aiden. And then where would she be?

"It's OK for friends to hold hands. Right?" Aiden's hesitation came through soft-spoken words.

"Yeah. Sure." Summer's heartbeat launched into overdrive.

He eased his hand around hers. The warmth and

gentleness of his touch sent a poignant longing through her. When he intertwined their fingers, Summer's entire body quaked. Aiden returned his gaze to the river, but she couldn't take her eyes off him.

Broad shoulders. Strong, angled jaw—he'd let his whiskers grow overnight. His thick dark hair lifted with the breeze. He was quite the specimen.

Of course, she'd noticed all those things the first time she'd seen him. But now that she knew a compassionate, masculine heart beat behind those features, she couldn't get enough, which could prove to be more dangerous to her well-being than any raging river or car accident.

The thought of the river reminded her she hadn't seen Zack for several minutes. She leaned forward and peeked around. He was nowhere in sight. But she could hardly go searching. Zack would know she hadn't trusted him to handle things on his own and their relationship was precarious already.

Aiden met her gaze. "I think I'll take a kayak downriver. Maybe run across Zack, see how he's holding up."

Summer let out a breath. "I would appreciate that. Maybe by the time his visit comes to an end, I'll have this worry thing under control. I just hope he stays out of trouble in the meantime."

"Don't count on it. I got into my fair share of mischief when I was his age."

"*No*. Not you." Summer playfully nudged Aiden's elbow. "Any details you care to share?"

"Just some harmless pranks."

"Like cow tipping?"

"Zack told you?" He chuckled as he released her hand and climbed to his feet. "So much for man-to-man confidentiality."

"It's one of the few things I didn't have to pry from his lips." Summer stood beside Aiden and then folded the chair. "Since you've got things covered out here, I'll head back inside and throw together a casserole for dinner." She hesitated. "Would you care to join us?"

"Thanks, but I'll probably be out on the river until late tonight. Besides, you two need some time together to get reacquainted."

"I wish it was as easy as having a meal with Zack. He's so different than the boy I used to know."

Aiden's brows rose. "Is there something I should know?"

She didn't want to tattle on Zack. This was supposed to be his fresh start, but Aiden might be able to help. "He's been arrested several times for stealing."

Aiden crossed his arms. "How much time has he spent in juvenile detention?"

"So far? None. And I hope to keep it that way. The problem is, his father's ex-partner won't be around to bail him out anymore."

"Maybe that's a good thing. If Zack doesn't suffer consequences for his actions, why would he ever stop? And, behaviors like that can often escalate."

"Well, when he returns home, if I haven't managed to straighten him out, he could get into deep trouble."

"If *you* haven't managed to straighten him out? That's a lot of responsibility you're placing on yourself. Don't you think?"

"I volunteered to take him in."

"And you're supposed to fix him on your own?"

"Not exactly. I've been praying for help."

"God sends people to help people. You're not alone in this, Summer. I'm here if you need me. What exactly do you think is going on?"

"I think his behavior has more to do with losing his father than anything else. As much as Riley tries to be there for Zack, she can't be the male role model he needs right now."

Aiden glanced toward the river. "Then maybe I should see what kind of influence I can have. That is, if you think it's a good idea?"

"You'd make a great mentor. But I couldn't ask that of you. You have your own life."

"You didn't ask. I'm volunteering. Maybe if we join forces, we'll get this kid back on track before he returns home."

And maybe, if Aiden kept this up, she'd be falling in love with him after all. "Then we'll be in this together."

"There's no other way I'd rather it be."

23

Summer plated the warm ham, cheese, and broccoli casserole and scooted it toward Zack.

He didn't seem to notice as he flipped through a skateboarding magazine at the kitchen bar. He still wore the same sweat jacket with the hood pulled over his head and had a pair of earbuds tucked in his ears.

She tapped him on the shoulder.

He unplugged his music. "Yeah?"

"Dinner."

He sniffed the casserole and plucked out a piece of broccoli.

"It's your grandma's secret recipe."

He looked skeptical, but inhaled his food and went for seconds before Summer finished preparing glasses of ice water.

"I'm glad you like it."

"Eh. It's OK." He kept his gaze on his plate.

Summer took a bite. The food tasted good, maybe a little too salty, but concern for Zack wilted her appetite.

After returning from the kayak trip earlier, he'd spent the next several hours alone in his room.

If they didn't start talking soon, she might not get through to him at all. She ate a couple more mouthfuls and then set aside her plate. "I really think we can have fun together this summer, if you'll give it a try."

"Maybe." He finished eating, rinsed the plate in the sink, and set it down. The hood on his head masked his features, but his tone sounded sullen and withdrawn.

"You can take off your jacket. Aren't you hot?"

"I always wear it."

"Your mother mentioned that." He'd even worn it beneath his lifejacket on the river. "Why?"

He turned to face her and she caught a glimpse of his eyes. "What's with the twenty questions?"

"I want you to be comfortable and happy here. Aiden thought maybe he could show you around Glade Springs sometime. Would you like him to?"

He shrugged, plugged back into his music, and flipped through the magazine again.

Lord, help me. I've never felt so unprepared in my life. Summer stored away the remainder of the casserole, cleaned the counter, and gathered the trash. Rather than asking for help, she took the bag outside herself. Zack could wait another day or two before pitching in with chores. She didn't bother to announce that she'd be right back. He wouldn't have heard her anyway.

She disposed of the bag in the dumpster Frank had tucked into a discreet corner next to the building and then gave herself a moment alone on the porch. Someone—probably Dottie—had added a variety of potted flowers on the edges, brightening the white wooden planks with colorful hues of baby blue, pale yellow, and deep violet. Summer touched a soft pedal, thankful to have Dottie as a neighbor. The woman had a knack for making The Meadows feel like home.

An owl hooted in a nearby tree and shadows danced in the darkness beyond the porch lights. Various creatures sang night songs. Proof of life was all around her and with it came a distinct knowledge that she wasn't in this alone. *Thank You, Lord, for Your plans to give us hope and a future…please show me what to do to help Zack.*

Summer lingered a few more minutes before entering the foyer. As she climbed the stairs, she met Devin on his way out. He had a tailored suit coat slung over an arm as he fiddled with the cuffs on his crisp white button-down shirt. He stopped and his musky cologne hung around him like a personal cloud. "You haven't seen any small boxes I might have dropped while moving in, have you?"

"No. Why?"

"I haven't been able to find my cufflinks since the move. I distinctly remember packing them, and I was sure I brought them inside. They were a gift from my father. They have my first initial and my last name inscribed on them."

"Have you unpacked everything?"

"Yes, and I'm not missing anything else."

He would know, as meticulous as he appeared with his possessions.

"Maybe the box dropped in the driveway, or it could be still in your car."

"That's what I'm hoping." His blond brows drew together. "Dad will be disappointed if I lost them. The diamonds alone are worth thousands."

"Wow. I didn't realize cufflinks could be so expensive. I'll let you know if I happen to see anything."

"I'd appreciate it. I've got to go. Catch you later." Devin swept past her, his cologne leaving a trail behind him.

Summer stifled a sneeze. She was glad Aiden didn't wear cologne. He didn't need it. He smelled good all on his own. Her thoughts shifted. She could see if Aiden had returned from his kayak trip. Maybe he could get Zack to talk. She detoured toward Aiden's door and knocked.

No answer came.

Oh, well. She could borrow Patches for a little while. Summer grinned. Nobody could resist Patches. She targeted Dottie's apartment. Within five minutes, she had Patches tucked under an arm and a peanut-butter-flavored dog bone in hand. When she returned to her apartment, Zack looked up from his perch on the barstool.

"What's that?"

"This is Patches. He's the friendliest Chihuahua ever."

Patches sniffed the air, caught a whiff of the bone, and whined for the treat.

Zack looked him over. "What'd you do? Find him by the dumpster?"

Summer sucked in an offended breath. "No. He's my neighbor's. I like to borrow him from time to time." She set down Patches and gave him the treat.

The dog gobbled the food, licked his lips, and searched for more.

Zack eased from the barstool, knelt, and petted Patches. "He is kind of cute."

A ray of hope sparked.

"For a mutt," he added.

"He's a purebred."

"Yeah. Whatever." Zack shuffled to his bedroom and shut the door.

"That's great." Summer shook her head, scooped up Patches. "Looks like it's time for reinforcements." She headed for the balcony, prepared to wait for Aiden to return.

24

As much as Aiden enjoyed spending nights on the river, he paddled back to The Meadows earlier than usual. He'd meant what he said about helping Zack. Growing up fatherless gave him a certain understanding of what Zack was facing. And to be honest with himself, he also hoped to spend some time with Summer.

Aiden reached the shore, stepped into the shallow water, and hefted the kayak over his shoulders. He made quick work of returning the boat to the storage shed and then jogged toward the building. Several new sets of flowers rested on the porch. Selecting a delicate violet flower, he picked it from the plant and stepped inside.

Once upstairs, Aiden approached Summer's apartment. He raised his hand to knock, but before he could, her door flung open and she grabbed him by his shirt.

"I need you." She yanked him inside.

"That's possibly the best welcome I've ever received." He considered going in for a kiss, but thought better of it as he took in her frazzled expression. "What's wrong?"

"It's Zack. I don't know what to do with him." She glanced at the flower in Aiden's hand and tilted her head. "Isn't that Dottie's?"

He suddenly felt like a thief. "I thought you might like it." He offered the flower, which now seemed a pitiable gesture compared to the large display of red roses showcased on her coffee table.

"Aww." A mixture of emotions crossed her features, ranging from antsy, to touched, and then back to worried again all in the span of two seconds. She accepted the flower and took a quick sniff. "Thanks."

"So, what's going on with Zack?" He followed her to the kitchen.

"Nothing. But that's the problem. After he came back from the river, I haven't been able to pry two words from him. I even borrowed Patches for a few minutes, but Zack wants nothing to do with either of us."

Aiden wanted to wrap his arms around Summer, but fully aware he'd been sweating most of the evening, he kept his distance. "Give him some time."

"I'm afraid I've stepped in over my head." She took up a dishcloth, wet it in the sink, and squeezed out excess water before scrubbing the counter. "I can't imagine an entire summer like this."

"Things will change." One way or another. Either Zack would open up a little, or he'd find more trouble to get into. Aiden chose to remain optimistic. "He'll come around."

"I don't want to keep bothering you with my problems. I don't want to interrupt your life."

Well, sweat or no sweat, he wasn't letting her get away with that comment. He gently prodded the dishcloth from her hand and drew her into a hug. "If I didn't want to be here, I wouldn't be."

Some of the stiffness left her shoulders. She relaxed against him and returned his embrace. "Are you always this nice?" she mumbled against his chest.

Aiden rested his chin on top of her head. "I have

my moments, just like anyone else. I'm liable to do something you don't agree with sooner or later."

"I'd rather it be later. I kind of like where we are at the moment."

"And where is that?" Was she hedging toward telling him something? His heart beat picked up pace. A door opening registered in the back of Aiden's mind, but he chose to ignore it. He nuzzled Summer's hair, enjoying her sweet, honeyed fragrance.

"Again?" Zack's voice cut through Aiden's thoughts. "How about giving me a warning next time you two want to make out?"

Summer ejected herself from Aiden's arms. "We weren't..." Her cheeks flushed into a crimson color. "He was just—"

"I stopped by to check on you two," Aiden said in a calm voice.

Zack uttered something unintelligible as he bypassed them and stuck his head into the fridge. "There's nothing to eat in this place."

"We just finished dinner." Summer tossed up her hands.

"Yeah. An hour ago." Zack rustled around and withdrew a gallon of milk. He made a move to drink from the container, but one stern look from Summer, and Zack changed his mind. He took out a cup instead. "I'm fifteen. I don't need a babysitter."

Aiden kept his stance and his expression neutral. "Never said you did. Actually, I was hoping you'd help me look after Summer. She's had a rough time of it lately."

Zack paused as if the possibility had never occurred to him. "What about?"

Aiden detailed the incident on the river and the

car accident. "She came too close to not being here with us." Chills raked his spine and his protective instincts surged forth again. He placed a hand at the small of her back, just because he wanted the contact.

A flicker of something other than annoyance shadowed Zack's deep brown eyes. "Mom said something about that." He turned to Summer. "But you're OK, right?"

"Yes. Thanks to Aiden. He rescued me on both counts."

"And now you're dating?" Zack chugged the milk, refilled his cup, and drank more.

"Not exactly." Summer found the dishcloth again. This time, she smoothed the kitchen faucet till it shined. "We're—"

"More than just friends," Aiden supplied. No use in denying the truth. He kept his gaze on Summer to judge her reaction. She avoided looking at him. He didn't want to make her uncomfortable, so he added, "But not quite to the girlfriend and boyfriend level yet."

Zack choked on his last sip of milk. "Could have fooled me."

Aiden crossed his arms and leaned on the counter. "We could talk about this all night, but I have a feeling you'd rather not."

"You got that right." Zack returned the milk container to the fridge, set down the cup, and swiped an arm across his lips. His cellphone chirped and he checked the screen before texting a reply. Keeping his gaze glued to the phone, he disappeared inside his room and shut the door.

"Well, so much for drawing him into a conversation." Aiden shook his head.

"You managed to get more out of him than I did. Maybe I should text him. I might get better results."

"Not a bad idea." Aiden relaxed his arms and tucked hands into his pockets. "If it's OK with you, will you ask him if he'd like to go on a tubing trip this weekend?"

Summer's eyes lit up. "Tubing? On the river?"

"Yeah. A couple of times during the season, I meet up with other firefighters and their families at River Run Outfitters and take an afternoon float trip. We pack a picnic lunch, take our time enjoying the river. It's always a blast. We're planning to go Saturday. I was hoping you and Zack would come."

"Oh, that sounds like fun. I haven't tried tubing yet. I never wanted to go alone."

"Now's your chance. There will be plenty of people in the group to hang out with."

"Hold on." Summer retrieved her cellphone and tapped the screen. "Let's see if Zack will answer me."

A moment later, a reply came and she read it. "He said OK." She grinned. "At least I know how to communicate with him now."

"It's a step in the right direction." Aiden enjoyed Summer's smile before worry lines creased her brows again. "What's wrong?"

"What if Zack has been texting his friends in New York? The ones Riley's trying to get him away from?"

"It's not a matter of what if. You can be certain he is. The question is, what kind of influence can they still have on him from so many miles away?"

25

River Run Outfitters sat nestled amongst a forest of trees and foliage that all but consumed the rustic check-in center.

Summer followed Aiden into the cabin-style building and Zack trailed behind. Country music played in the background, and although several windows allowed in light, the dim interior contrasted with the brilliant sunshine outdoors.

The young clerk at the front desk recognized Aiden and greeted him by name. As Aiden filled out necessary paperwork, Summer glanced around the small, equipment-filled room. Various camping and hiking accessories filled shelves, ranging from bug spray and sunscreen to maps and first-aid equipment. She sauntered toward a display of backpacks hanging on the far wall.

"I'm going to wait outside." Zack disappeared through the screen door.

At least he'd agreed to come.

Summer couldn't expect him to be thrilled, as this type of thing was way out of his normal routine. But she hoped he'd end up having a good time.

She glanced at Aiden, and her heart skipped a beat. He looked at home in this environment. His bright-blue swim trunks complemented the T-shirt he wore, and his black water shoes finished off the ensemble. But it wasn't his clothes that captured her attention—it was the easy smile on his face. As his gaze met hers, his eyes sparkled with excitement. Aiden winked and she nearly tripped over her own feet.

Self-conscious, she adjusted the shirt covering her emerald-green swimsuit and tugged at the pair of matching swim shorts. With the added protection of sunscreen coating her skin, she was prepared, at least physically. Emotionally, she wasn't sure she'd be ready at all. She'd be spending the day with Aiden and his coworkers. She'd met a few of his friends at the firehouse, and a few more when she'd been rescued from her overturned car. But she'd yet to spend an extended length of time with them. Would she fit in with the group? Or would they consider her an outsider?

Aiden left his truck's key with the clerk and headed her way. "You ready? The equipment we need is outside. I reserved tubes with the seat bottoms in them. Thought you might prefer those to the open kind."

The fact Aiden considered her comfort settled her nerves a little. But not enough. As they stepped out and found the remainder of the crew had arrived, she hesitated. "Wow. That's a lot of people."

Aiden placed a hand at the small of her back. "Don't worry. They'll love you."

Encouraged, she took the three steps to the graveled parking lot and made her way through introductions.

Marilyn, the woman she'd met at the fire station and the one she'd seen on the TV news broadcast dashing out of the burning house, stepped forward first with two kids in tow and a lanky husband wearing rounded glasses. "It's nice to see you again." The woman's hazel eyes warmed as she shook hands with Summer. "This is Trevor, my eleven-year-old son."

Summer nodded at the boy, who danced from foot to foot as if anxious to get on the water.

"And this is Kayla. My oldest."

Kayla, a pretty blonde looking to be about Zack's age, offered her soft hand in a shake. "Nice to meet you."

Marilyn's husband introduced himself next and then several more people passed by with brief introductions. Summer counted about thirty in all and her mind spun with names and faces. "I hope they don't expect me to remember every name."

Aiden's hand had remained on her back the entire time, and now he smoothed his palm along her spine. The sensation made her tremble. In a good way.

"It's a lot to take in all at once, I know. But I'll help you with names. Just ask."

And she did. As they situated lifejackets and climbed onto the shuttle bus, Summer asked Aiden names and she tried to memorize them. All in all, there were eight other firefighters, each with several family members. She remembered a few names and resolved to let the rest go.

Aiden and Zack squeezed Summer between them on the bench seat and Summer leaned toward Zack. "If you want to hang out with the others your age, feel free, just remember to stay with the group."

His brown eyes darted toward Kayla. "We'll see."

Summer's hopes spiraled. If he could make one friend today, the entire trip would be a success.

As the bus jostled along a narrow dirt road, Summer bumped against Aiden. Sitting shoulder to shoulder, thigh to thigh, brought on a new kind of anticipation. Even in the stuffy bus, Aiden's masculine scent ruled her senses.

Aiden took her hand in his and intertwined their fingers. "This is beginning to feel like a date." He held her gaze as if challenging her to pull away.

She should disentangle her hand from his. After all, she still hadn't officially agreed to date him. But having him near muddled her thoughts.

"Relax." He smoothed a thumb along the back of her hand. "You don't have to figure it all out today."

He was right. She didn't have to plan her entire future while tubing the Shenandoah River. She didn't have to know what would happen between her and Aiden to enjoy the day. For possibly the first time she could remember, she allowed herself to live in the moment.

After a bumpy ride, they arrived at the drop-off location, which consisted of a small parking area and a long, narrow beach. The shuttle driver helped offload the tubes, and Aiden tied an extra tube to his and set a cooler and various picnic items inside.

Thankful Aiden had taken care of the necessities, Summer found her tube and waded into the cool river. After making certain Zack was settled and ready to float, she climbed onto her cheery yellow inner tube.

Within minutes, the entire group was headed downriver, floating at a slow but steady pace. With the various bright-colored inner tubes spreading out, the group as a whole looked like one big dotted rainbow decorating the river.

Aiden paddled alongside her, grasped her tube's handle, and held them side by side. "What do you think so far?"

"I'm used to having to paddle the kayak. This is so

relaxing." She laid back her head and allowed the warm sun to melt away any remaining tension as the water flowed around her ankles.

"I'm glad you're enjoying yourself. Looks like Zack's having a good time, too."

Summer shielded her eyes from the sun and searched for his turquoise tube. He'd found a group of teenagers to hang around. "Could have something to do with the pretty young woman he's found to admire."

"I know the feeling." Aiden captured her gaze and his blatant admiration melted her insides.

She wanted to accept all he offered. But even though she'd vowed to live in the moment today, tomorrow would come all too soon and with it, consequences.

"I'll be back in a few." Aiden flashed a quick, heart-stopping smile and released his hold, allowing their tubes to drift apart as he visited with other firefighters.

Summer enjoyed observing his interactions with those he called his family. He engaged them in conversation, sometimes smiling and laughing, always emphatic. Several times, she caught him glancing her way, as if he'd been discussing his relationship with her to the others.

"It might be none of my business"—Marilyn used her hands as paddles and eased alongside Summer— "but it is good to see Aiden showing an interest in someone. You're the first woman he's ever brought tubing. I hope you share the same feelings as he obviously has for you."

Summer appreciated the woman's protective nature, as if she had a vested interest in Aiden's happiness. "Honestly, I'm fighting against it, but I don't know how long I can hold out."

"Why resist? Are you involved with someone else?"

"No. It's not that." If anyone could give her insight, this woman could. "I'm wary of dating a man in a risky profession."

Understanding lit her features. "It happens, but love overcomes a lot of things."

"How does your husband feel about you being a firefighter?"

Marilyn smiled, a compassionate gesture more than anything. "As an accountant with about as safe a job as you can get, Joseph had a difficult adjustment at first. But he came around."

"How? Isn't he still worried every time you go to work? What about your kids?"

"The kids don't know any different. I've been a firefighter since long before they were born. And as far as Joseph is concerned, he used to worry each time I went to work. Eventually, he got used to the idea. Sometimes I text him to let him know what's going on, sometimes he has to wait until I get home to know I'm OK. Over time, he's learned to trust me. But most importantly, he has learned to trust God with me."

Marilyn's words struck a chord. Aiden had asked for her trust, and she was working on that, but trusting God *with* Aiden...well, that was entirely different. Aiden hadn't chosen his profession on a whim. He'd been called to be a firefighter. And what safer place could Aiden be than in God's will?

An unprecedented sense of hope blanketed Summer with warmth that not even the sun's hot rays could provide.

"Looks like your nephew is fond of my daughter." Marilyn's comment brought Summer from her thoughts. The woman's astute hazel eyes zoned in on Zack as he hung out near Kayla. "I hope he's a good kid."

"Deep down, he is," Summer answered on instinct. "I'm hoping his visit here will help him remember how happy he was before he lost his father."

"Well, if a long stay in Shenandoah Valley doesn't bring Zack to realize his blessings, nothing else will."

"Very true." This visit might just prove to be a vital turning point in his life. *Thank You, Lord, for this day. Although things can never be the same for Zack again, help him find the hope and peace he needs to fulfill the calling You have on his life.*

"Well, I'd better check on my youngest." Marilyn excused herself and the current separated them.

Summer floated where nature directed. She called greetings to those she neared, made small talk with some, while simply waving at others.

"I see a smile on your face. Having fun?" Aiden splashed his way over.

Summer warmed at his familiar voice. "Absolutely. Thanks for thinking of us."

"Lately, you're all I think about." His tender words matched his softened expression. Before Summer could respond or even absorb his words, Aiden hitched his chin in Zack's direction. "I think it's time for a water fight. What do you say? You approach from the left and I'll flank the right side. We'll get Zack and anyone else in between."

"You're on." Giddiness rose up inside as if she'd reverted to a kid again. "I'll race you."

26

"Riley, you won't believe the day we've had." Summer held her cellphone tight against her ear as she finished dressing after a shower. The trip had been long, and she was exhausted but exhilarated at the same time.

"Uh-oh. What did Zack do? Do I need to come pick him up?" Riley's voice sounded world weary, withdrawn, and hesitant.

"No, it's not like that. Zack's doing great. Aiden took us on a tubing trip on the Shenandoah River with some of his firefighter buddies and their families. Zack made new friends today." Summer smoothed on after-sun lotion, careful not to irritate her pink shoulders. "We were out all afternoon. We had a great time."

"Really? Tell me about Zack's friends."

"Their names are Kayla, Robbie, and Stuart. Aiden knows their parents. He says they're all good kids, and if today was any indication, they've adopted him into their gang." She cringed. Not the best choice of words. "I meant that as a good thing." Some other teens had hung close by, but Summer noticed the little group was especially tight-knit. "Zack managed to get Kayla's phone number. He's got a date with her tonight. I hope that's OK with you."

"It's fantastic. If I was there, I'd be hugging you so tight right now. I can't tell you how much this means to me. Thank you so much."

"You should thank Aiden. The trip was his idea."

He'd shared his family with her today, and before the trip had ended, she'd been unofficially adopted into the clan.

"How are things going with you two? Was today a date?" Rustling sounds came over the phone, and Summer imagined Riley settling onto her chaise lounge.

"Aiden mentioned something about today feeling like a date."

"So it wasn't an official date? Why is this moving along so slow?"

"Because of me." Summer wasn't sure if she should delve into this now, but with her relationship with Aiden progressing, Riley was bound to catch on sooner or later. "I told him I didn't date men in risky careers." She held her breath.

Certainly, Riley would understand, but would it bring back the pain?

Riley huffed. "You can't be serious. Are you afraid to date Aiden because of what happened to Doug?"

"Yes." Summer exhaled. She might sound like a coward but her fears were justified. Finished with the aloe, she exited her bathroom. Zack had already left, so Summer could talk freely. "I saw how heartbroken you were—"

"Summer Rose Cassel. You listen to me." Riley used that mothering tone Summer had learned to respect. "I cherish every moment I had with Doug. We had our ups and downs like anyone else, but I would not give up one second of the time I had with him to spare myself the grief of losing him. And, if Aiden is half as good a man as you've made him out to be, you'd better not let him slip through your fingers."

Summer sank onto her couch. Her resolve

wavered, but fear reared its ugly head. "A part of me wants to give this a try, but I'm scared. I'm afraid he's the one guy I could fall so deeply in love with, if I lost him, I'm not sure I'd live through it."

"God won't let anything happen to you that you can't handle with His help. He's seen me through the darkest months, placing people in my life to help me as needed. He would do the same for you if something like that happened. And I'm not saying that it would." She took in a deep breath. "Don't let fear rule your decisions. And certainly don't let it keep you from the happiness you deserve."

Summer sat idle as she contemplated Riley's words. The only sounds in the apartment came from the washing machine as it twirled and swished the bathing suits and towels they'd used that day. And even those noises fell silent as if in respect for the situation's gravity.

She didn't have all the answers but she did know one thing. "I want to be happy."

"Then don't push Aiden away. What if he's the man God intends for you?"

What if Aiden was that man and she refused him? He had admirable qualities. He'd proven himself to be kind, generous, strong, and courageous. And, just looking at him made her knees grow weak and her insides flutter. "I'll think about it."

"You think too much. Follow your heart."

"When did you get so wise?"

"Years of practice. I am a decade older than you." The connection blipped and Riley sighed. "I've got another call coming through. I need to take it. Let me know how things turn out. And give Zack a hug for me."

Summer mulled over Riley's advice. Her sister had never been one to hold back thoughts, and in this case, Summer appreciated the insight. Would things have been different from the start if she'd known Riley had no regrets about marrying a man in a dangerous profession? Would she have welcomed Aiden's advances with open arms? For the first time, she seriously considered moving forward with Aiden and allowing their friendship to develop into something more. *Lord, I know You have good plans for me. Forgive me for letting worry rule my life. Help me to make decisions based on faith instead of fear.*

The clothes washer kicked into the spin cycle and then a few minutes later, buzzed, indicating it had finished. Summer used the timing as an excuse to stop thinking altogether. She needed to give this new information a chance to digest, and routine housework was just what she needed. She climbed from the couch and hung the bathing suits in the bathroom, while placing the towels into the dryer. As she gathered dirty clothes to start another load, she walked past Zack's room. His gray hoodie hung on the door. He'd actually taken it off for his evening with Kayla.

"That's amazing," Summer announced to the empty apartment as she picked up the jacket by the hood and took a sniff. "Ick." The musty material needed a thorough washing. It took Summer all of one second to make up her mind. She'd have Zack's treasured jacket clean and dry before he returned.

She made her way to the washer, automatically checking to make sure the hoodie's pockets were empty. She found nothing on the left side, but when she dug into the right, her fingers collided with some small objects. She grasped them and took them out.

Two gold cufflinks adorned with multiple diamonds sat in her palm.

She recalled her conversation with Devin. He was missing a set of cufflinks and Zack had been inside Devin's apartment. Coincidence? She could only hope. She turned the cufflinks around, giving them a closer inspection. An inscription on the back read *D. Paxton.*

The hoodie slipped through her fingers and fell to the floor. Zack had done it again. This time, he'd stolen from under her nose. Her mouth dried and she swallowed stark disappointment like a bitter medicine, nearly choking. Is this what Riley had been experiencing all this time?

Riley would know what to do. Summer headed for her cellphone, but stilled halfway to her purse. Riley had been so relieved to hear things were going well. Tomorrow would come soon enough. She'd tell her then.

She could confront Zack when he returned home, but waiting around until ten o'clock—assuming he would observe his curfew—seemed impossible. What if Devin had filed a police report about the missing cufflinks? Could she return them and convince Devin not to press charges? Surely, he would understand. Then again, he hadn't seemed especially tolerant of kids. How would he react to a juvenile delinquent? And Summer admitted with a heavy heart, that a delinquent was what Zack had become.

Tears burned the backs of her eyes. As if the stolen objects carried a curse on them, the cufflinks burned her palms. She had to return them before this situation grew any worse. She tugged down the hem of her tank top and adjusted her cotton capri lounge pants. Her casual attire would do nothing to help her cause, but she didn't want to take the time to change into something nicer. Exiting her apartment, Summer made a beeline for Devin's door. She knocked, and when he didn't answer within five seconds, she pounded harder.

Nothing happened. Not even a sound emerged.

"Devin. Are you home?" she called out.

A door's soft click sounded nearby.

"What's going on?" Aiden's voice registered.

Summer spun around. He stood in the threshold of his apartment, wearing a pair of jeans, a navy fire department T-shirt, and a wary expression.

"You look as if you've seen a ghost." His brows drew together.

Summer hadn't thought to involve Aiden, but since he was standing only a few yards away, she could hardly hide her distress. "I need to talk to Devin. Do you know when he'll be back?"

"I have no idea." Aiden allowed his door to close and strode toward her. "Seriously. You don't look well. What's happening?"

"I…" She could handle this herself another time or tell Aiden what she'd found. If she shut him out, she could very well injure their tentative relationship. And he was there again when she needed support. Maybe Riley was right. She needed to give him a chance.

Aiden placed his hands on her shoulders, piercing her with an imploring gaze. "Let me help you."

How could she deny him? She steeled her shaky nerves. "I found these in Zack's pocket." She opened her palm to reveal the cufflinks. "He stole them from Devin."

Aiden picked up the items. "These must be worth a lot of money."

"Devin was looking for them earlier this week and asked me if I'd seen them. Zack helped transfer a few boxes from Devin's car. The cufflinks might have been in one of them." Desperation seeped through her voice. "Riley provides Zack with everything he needs. Why does he keep stealing things?"

"I don't know. But it's time we find out." Aiden pocketed the cufflinks. "I'm assuming Zack isn't home?"

"No. He went to a movie with Kayla."

"I'm going after him."

"Wait." Summer grasped his arm. "I'll come with you."

"It would be better if you stay here. You can call me if he comes home."

Waiting around for something to happen wasn't her first choice, but what he said made sense. "What are you going to do when you find him?"

A muscle ticked in Aiden's jaw. "Whatever it takes to keep this from ever happening again."

27

Summer had exhausted her patience. Aiden had spun wheels out of the parking lot two hours ago, and she'd yet to hear a word. She wished there was some other plausible explanation for the cufflinks being in Zack's pocket, but she had yet to think of one good reason. She needed to talk to him. She had to set things straight.

Desperate, she called Zack's cellphone but he didn't answer. She texted him but he didn't reply.

Summer picked up the rental car's keys and stepped toward the door. But Aiden's words reverberated. If Zack came home, she would need to be here. She set down the keys again and paced. She twisted the ruby ring around her finger and glanced at the clock. Zack's curfew was approaching. He'd be home soon. Or would he?

The house phone rang, making her tense muscles jerk. Aiden or Zack would call her cellphone. Who else would be calling so late? Her gut churned as she picked up the receiver. "Hello?"

"Ms. Cassel?" The man's voice wasn't familiar.

"Yes? Who is this?"

"This is Deputy Kershaw with the Glade Springs Sheriff's Department. We have Zack Billings in custody. Are you his guardian?"

Summer struggled for breath. Her lungs refused to cooperate and it took her a moment to respond. "Yes. I'm responsible for him until the end of August. Why is he there?" She squeezed her eyes shut. She didn't really want to know.

The deputy cleared his throat. "Well, ma'am, he has stolen valuable personal property from Dr. Devin Paxton, and also Mr. Aiden Hawk. We need you to come..."

The deputy's words turned into a blur in her mind. No surprise about Devin's possessions, but what had Zack stolen from Aiden? Her tongue felt thick and heavy as she managed to reply, "I'll be there as soon as I can."

If Aiden was involved and knew what was happening, why hadn't he called her directly? Summer flipped off her living room lights and headed out the door. Checking her cellphone, she jogged to the parking lot. No new messages or missed calls. She dialed Aiden's number, but he didn't answer. *Lord, help me.*

On the drive into town, she had to curb her speed every so often—it would do Zack no good for her to get in another accident. She had to be levelheaded. She had to be strong even though her insides quivered with dread.

Summer kept her hands tight on the wheel as she approached Glade Springs's business district. The town's main road held various establishments, including a bank, a couple of hardware stores, and a real estate office, all of which looked as if they'd been in operation for decades. Normally, Summer enjoyed the scenery, imagining days gone by in this area rich with history. But today she passed by without really seeing anything other than the sheriff's station looming ahead. The square, red-brick building sat on a low rise at the town's far end, directly across the street from the courthouse. Would she be heading there next? The thought caused her stomach to revolt.

Aiden's truck sat parked in the lot, and Summer pulled in next to it. She should be relieved he was there, but considering Zack had stolen from him too, her nerves stretched even farther.

Summer stumbled through the station's double doors, squinting at the bright fluorescent lights overhead. Lingering scents of coffee permeated the stuffy room. A young deputy sat at the front desk with a phone to his ear and a pencil in hand. He scribbled something on a paper, glanced at her, and then held up a finger as if Summer had the time to wait.

She stifled the urge to interrupt the man's conversation. She didn't say anything, but sighed and tapped her foot on the linoleum floor. A few desks sat scattered about and several doors led to other areas. A long hallway in the back led to what could be holding cells or maybe interrogation rooms.

"Summer."

She started at the sound of her name. Aiden appeared in a doorway to what she assumed was an office. He motioned her inside with a quick flip of his wrist, his expression somber.

She'd never seen him so serious. This was so not good. Summer skirted the desks and headed toward the office.

Sheriff Alvin Craigen's name was stenciled in gold-leaf lettering on the glass-paneled door. She followed Aiden as he returned inside.

Devin stood from one of the chairs opposite the sheriff's empty desk, his amber eyes filled with uncertainty. "Summer. I had hoped we could resolve this on our own. But Aiden is insisting—"

"Hold on." Aiden cut him off, hands raised. "Let's back up a minute so I can explain what's going on." He met Summer's gaze. "On my way into town, I discovered some of my music CDs missing from my truck."

"That doesn't mean Zack stole them." Summer shook her head. Sheer despair had her rooting for explanations. "Anyone could have—"

Aiden stepped close, touched a hand to her elbow, and lowered his voice. "I called Marilyn to find out where she'd dropped off Zack and Kayla. She told me the name of the movie and the time it was playing. When the movie ended, Zack took Kayla to a pawn shop instead of calling Marilyn to pick them up. I followed them, intending to take Zack aside and talk to him in private, but when I stepped inside, he was trying to sell my CDs. He was also asking about the value of gold cufflinks with diamonds."

The information was too much, too fast. Overwhelmed, dizziness ensued. Summer searched for a place to sit.

Devin stepped aside and offered his seat.

She sank onto the hard plastic chair, wishing the office had better air conditioning. She could scarcely breathe in the warm, humid room. "What did you do after that?"

Aiden stood over her, his expression stoic. "I called Marilyn. She picked up Kayla and took her home. I brought Zack here."

"W-why?" Summer gripped the seat's armrests so hard her knuckles protested. "Why didn't you bring him to me? We could've sorted all this out ourselves."

"That's the last thing Zack needs. He won't—"

Aiden's words were cut short as the sheriff—a

burly man with a lengthy mustache and a receding hairline—sauntered into the room. His steel-gray eyes zeroed in on Summer. "Ms. Cassel, I presume?" He held out a thick hand.

Summer didn't trust her legs to hold her, so she numbly shook his hand without standing. "Where's Zack? I want to see him."

"Not tonight, ma'am." Sheriff Craigen edged around his desk and situated himself in the leather chair. "He's in a holding cell all settled in for the night."

"You make it sound as if he's checked into a hotel. He's in jail." She leaned forward. "I want him released."

"The earliest that could happen is tomorrow. But even then, that would be up to Aiden. He's the one pressing charges."

She whirled on Aiden. "*What*?"

No denial formed on his lips.

A profound sense of betrayal struck hard and swift. "How could you?"

"It's for the best." Aiden took a step toward her.

She held up a hand to ward him off. "How is it for the best? It was a couple of CDs. I would think if anyone would press charges, it would be Devin."

Devin cleared his throat and fumbled with the tie constricting his neck. "I just want my cufflinks back. I don't want any trouble."

Aiden gave him a disparaging look. "You mean you don't want to bother to help get this kid straightened out."

Devin swallowed, looking to the sheriff for a reprieve. "If I'm finished here, I'd like to go home. I have plans tomorrow."

Sheriff Craigen nodded and shoved paperwork across the desk. "Sign here. Date here." He pointed to two blank lines.

Devin signed.

The sheriff handed over the cufflinks. "Thanks for coming in on such short notice."

"Not a problem." Devin looked at Summer. "I'll talk to you later."

Once he left, the sheriff smoothed long fingers over his mustache and fumbled with more papers. "Aiden, I'll need you to sign this one. Unless you've changed your mind about pressing charges?"

Aiden met Summer's gaze.

"Please don't." She cringed at the desperation in her voice.

He eased onto the chair next to her. "The last thing I want to do is hurt you." His voice came out raspy and apologetic. "But, this is what Zack needs."

"I thought we were friends. I thought you cared."

"I'm doing this *because* I care." He stared at her for so long she thought he might give in. But he didn't. He turned, picked up a pen, and signed the document.

Summer sprang from the chair and fled the confined office before the tears burning the backs of her eyes could find release.

~*~

Aiden's chest squeezed so tight he struggled to breathe. He dated his signature and dropped the pen on the desk. He gave the sheriff a curt nod. "I'll be back tomorrow to sort this out."

The sheriff leaned forward, clasping his hands. "Everyone in this town knows you're an upstanding citizen. You've proven that time and again. You are doing the right thing."

"Yeah, well, I hope Summer sees that before it's too late." Otherwise, his dreams of a future with her would be very short-lived. As it was, he feared he'd burned the very bridge he'd just begun to build with her. He had to catch up to her. He had to make her understand. "I've got to go."

"Good luck." The sheriff's parting words did nothing to soothe Aiden's inner turmoil.

Luck had no part in this. He needed God's intervention. *Lord, help me sort this out...*

He hoped to find Summer in the parking lot, but she'd already sped away by the time he stepped outside. He climbed into his truck, cranked the ignition, and slammed his foot on the accelerator. He caught sight of her on the outskirts of town and eased his speed, following at a safe distance.

When they arrived at The Meadows, Summer bounded from her rented car and Aiden had to run to catch up. He took hold of her elbow as she reached the foyer's double doors. "Please, wait."

She stopped and spun around so fast he almost ran into her. "I can't believe you're doing this." The porch lighting illuminated her flushed face, and she swiped hands over tear-stained cheeks. "You said that we were in this together. You said you would do whatever it takes." She took in a quick, shallow breath as her eyes widened. "Did you plan this all along? When you left my apartment, did you intend to take Zack to the sheriff?"

He hadn't had a plan at that point, other than talking to Zack, but he doubted Summer would believe him if he told her that now. "I didn't know what would happen."

"But you want him to pay for taking your things, don't you?"

"It's not about the CDs. Zack needs to experience consequences or he won't change his behavior."

Summer glanced at the fingers still clamped around her elbow.

He released her, and then smoothed a hand down her arm.

She pulled away.

Aiden's heart lodged in his throat. "Summer—"

"I can't do this now. I need time to think."

He needed a resolution. Tonight. One way or another. "Just like you needed time to think about us? It's time you stop letting fear lead your decisions."

"About us? Or about Zack?"

"Both." He paused, letting her soak in the implications. "I want you. I'm willing to wait for you. But sooner or later, I'll need to know what *you* want. And, as far as your nephew? Zack needs tough love right now, and if you're not willing or able to give it, then someone else has to step in and do it for you."

Recoiling as if he'd struck her, Summer's face paled and her lower lip trembled.

Regret slammed into him—she had voiced concerns about not being able to handle Zack and he'd pounced on her insecurities without thought. "Summer...I'm..." He stepped toward her.

Backing out of reach, Summer held up her palms. "You have some nerve telling me how to handle my nephew when you don't have any experience to back you up. You don't have any children. You've never even had a real family."

Aiden flinched. As if she'd severed nerve endings,

numbness stole over him. Blood rushed through his ears as his heart pounded. Beat after beat, he stood waiting for something, anything to alleviate his deep-rooted pain. But even time couldn't heal some wounds.

Somehow, he managed to whisper, "If you were looking for a way to hurt me, you found it."

28

Summer tossed and turned, tangling sheets as sleep evaded her. The Bible said not to let the sun go down on anger. And for good reason. The argument with Aiden played over in her mind like an endless record. What he'd said, what she'd said. What neither of them should have said.

Aiden had warned her that one day he'd do something she didn't like. Well, that day had come. But she should never have spoken of his lack of a family. She'd been hurt and lashed out, sought retribution. He'd reared back as if she'd plunged a knife into his chest and then twisted the blade.

Summer pounded a fist into her pillow, turned onto her side, and lay still, but her eyes refused to shut. The numbers on her digital clock glowed red in the dark bedroom. One o'clock and her exhausted body refused her sleep. She couldn't take back the words she'd spewed out, but she owed Aiden an apology. She ground her teeth. *Lord, do I have to do this now?* Yeah, she did. No need to listen for an answer she already knew.

She threw off the bedcovers and climbed to her feet. The air conditioner cranked out ice-cold air and she slipped into a robe, yanking the tie around her midsection. Aiden was probably asleep by now, but she couldn't get any rest without speaking to him—which fueled a frustration she couldn't contain.

Stomping across the living room, Summer exited

her apartment and targeted his door. She rammed her fist against the wood, not caring about the ruckus she created. "Aiden. We need to talk."

Footsteps sounded beyond the door. The latch gave way and Aiden peeked out with red-rimmed eyes. His tussled hair stuck out at odd angles as if he'd been raking fingers through it. "You can't sleep either?"

His soft-spoken words cooled her flames. She exhaled and her shoulders slumped. "No."

Opening the door wider, he stepped aside as if offering an invitation to enter.

She remained where she stood. If she crossed the threshold into his apartment, she'd be on his turf. No need to give him an edge. "I came over to..." The apology stuck on her tongue. "I wanted..." Oh, she'd have better success prying Aiden's tight-set jaw apart with a toothpick than opening her own mouth to say, "I'm sorry."

As if he understood her preference, Aiden stepped into the hallway, meeting her in neutral territory. He crossed his arms over his chest, probably because his drawstring sweatpants didn't have pockets for his hands. Without speaking, he assessed her with those lethally gorgeous eyes—eyes that drew her in like no other. It was so unfair. How could such a strong attraction blindside her after the night they'd had? Sometimes matters of the heart made no sense whatsoever.

She needed to get this done. Fast. "I apologize for what I said about you not having a family. It was awful of me, and I didn't mean it." There. She'd said it. Now maybe she could get some sleep. She turned and aimed for her apartment.

Aiden's grip on her arm halted her quick getaway. "Oh. No. You. Don't. You don't get to relieve your conscience and then run."

With her back still to him, she grimaced. "I can't make you accept my apology. I can only offer it. And I did."

"I do accept your apology." Moving in close, his breath skimmed her neck. "And you're trying to escape before I can offer mine."

Goose bumps sprang to life. His close proximity took its toll on her senses. His clean, masculine scent followed his every movement as he circled around to stand before her. No way would she let this physical attraction sidetrack the moment. "What exactly are you sorry about? Pressing charges?"

"No. I haven't and I won't change my mind about what I think is best for Zack. But, I am sorry for using your insecurities against you. It was not intentional."

"I didn't think it was." He wasn't the type to take advantage. "So, where does that leave us now?"

"That depends on you." Aiden cupped her face with his palms. He tilted up her chin as he drew closer; close enough to feel warmth radiating from his body, and close enough for the pleading in his eyes to register. "Will you trust me?"

Oh no. Not the *t* word. She could handle the *f* word better than the *t* word. Friends meant having someone to lean on for support. Trust meant letting go of fears. Was Aiden asking for both trust and friendship? No. He hadn't just wanted to be friends anymore. He'd made that clear. Even now, he dropped his gaze to her lips as if he wanted to kiss her.

Summer cleared her suddenly dry throat. "When you forgive, you do it without reservations, don't you?"

"It's the only way."

"Yeah, well. I forgive you too. But I'm still upset. Zack's in a jail cell tonight."

"I have a plan." His thumbs smoothed over her skin. "Please hear me out."

"A p-plan?" His touch made it hard to think clearly. She'd been tired after the tubing trip, and then the emotional roller coaster of discovering Zack's thievery and all of the night's events had exhaustion dogging her heels. It would be easy to succumb to the comfort and support Aiden offered. "What kind of plan?"

"The kind that gives Zack what he needs and both of us what we want."

"Sounds too good to be true."

"That's where the trust comes in." He let his hands fall to his sides and took a step back.

In spite of her reservations, she missed his gentle touch. She hugged her arms around her middle to fill the sudden void. "How so?"

"Glade Springs's juvenile court judge attends the same church that I do. I've spent enough time with Judge Harrison to know he's a fair and honest man. In the morning, I'll talk to him and explain Zack's situation. I'm going to suggest he sentence Zack to community service instead of jail time."

"What makes you think he will agree?"

"He's a man of faith, and he prays before making decisions. I'm confident he will do what's best for Zack."

"Maybe, but it still sounds risky to me."

"It's a risk worth taking."

Summer spun her ring in circles. "That's easy for

you to say. You don't have anything to lose."

"Oh yes, I do." Aiden's meaning came through clear as his gaze swept over her.

She hadn't even decided yet whether she'd date him, but now wasn't the time for that discussion. The recent wounds were too raw, too intense.

She reined in her focus. "Supposing your idea does work, what kind of community service are you talking about? I don't want Zack on the side of the road picking up trash."

"It's nothing like that. I want Zack to serve his time with me. We have plenty of service opportunities at the fire station. We'll be visiting Hope Haven Children's Home soon. He can ride along. Maybe he'll realize how blessed he is to have a family that loves him."

"And if he doesn't? What if he keeps stealing?"

"Then we'll cross that bridge when we get to it." Aiden reached for pockets that weren't there and then crossed his arms again. "I told you I would help. And I will. When I start something, I finish it."

She had no doubt he meant what he said. His betrayal hadn't been a betrayal after all. He'd had a plan all along. Summer released a pent-up breath, and as if he sensed her acceptance, the tension between them dissolved. "Zack does need to learn from his wrong choices. One way or another. Why are you doing this for him? For me?"

"Because I care about you."

Yeah, he'd proven that already. She should return the declaration. In spite of their disagreement, she had fallen a little bit more for him tonight.

Waiting patiently for her to say something, Aiden remained silent.

"I…" *I'm falling in love with you.* She couldn't finish the words as anxiety gripped her soul. Fears had dug her into a hole so deep she didn't know how to climb out. Losing Aiden now would be devastating. Losing him if they were together, in a permanent arrangement, would be catastrophic.

29

Aiden stepped out of Brookside Community Church and into the bright sun, intent on catching up to Judge Harrison. He hadn't had a chance before the service to speak with him, and Aiden had heard little of the pastor's sermon. He'd been too busy rehearsing how he'd approach the judge with the subject of Zack's future.

This had to work. Summer needed him. He'd admitted last night that he cared, but he didn't let on how much. When she'd knocked on his door, he'd been on his knees praying for a resolution. The fact she'd come to him and apologized had spoken volumes about her strength of character and her faith. Not just any woman would have sought restoration at all, much less so quickly. Aiden's resolve to keep his emotions in check had slipped, and his heart had crossed into a danger zone. Summer held a certain power over him, even more so than before. *Father, help me know the words to say. And please help Judge Harrison to be receptive to my ideas. If not, I could lose Summer's fragile trust, and I need that trust to finally win her over.*

Aiden swiped damp palms across his pants—it would do no good to let the judge detect how nervous he'd become. He crossed the parking lot and approached Judge Harrison before he entered his vehicle. "I'm glad I caught you before you left."

The judge whirled around and his ruddy face beamed a smile. "Aiden. It's good to see you. Saved any lives lately?"

"A couple." Aiden shook the man's hand. "I was hoping I could have a word with you. Do you have time to spare?" He bent low and offered Judge Harrison's wife a greeting as she waited in the passenger seat.

She nodded. "Why don't you join us for lunch? We're heading over to the diner for some grilled burgers."

"I don't want to intrude."

"Nonsense." Judge Harrison waved a hand. "We would enjoy the company."

"Well, if you're sure. I'd love to."

After following the Harrisons to the small diner located on the northern tip of Glade Springs, Aiden settled in at a table overlooking the Blue Ridge Mountains. The couple sat opposite him, and after a few minutes of small talk, Aiden delved into the details that led up to Zack's arrest. Each time he mentioned Summer's name, his heart beat a little faster. Did his emotional involvement show on his face?

It probably had, as Mrs. Harrison looked on him with compassion. She nudged her husband. "Isn't there something you can do, Edward?"

Aiden appreciated her concern, and he hadn't even asked for help yet. "I was hoping we could settle this without going to court. If you'll allow me to take personal responsibility for Zack, I'll make sure he gets the mentoring he so desperately needs."

Judge Harrison rubbed the nape of his neck. "So, you're the one pressing charges, but you want me to make arrangements to release him to your custody?"

"He can perform community service at the fire station. I'll keep an eye on him, and he can learn some responsibility."

"Why are you willing to do this?"

Aiden leaned forward, holding his gaze steady. "My calling in life to help people doesn't end when I finish my shift. I believe I can help Zack. All I'm asking is that you help me make a difference in his life."

"And?" He tilted his head as if sensing more to the story.

Aiden couldn't blame the man for digging for motives. It was his job. He thought for a moment about how much to reveal. He could mention that Zack was Summer's responsibility and he wanted to help her because he cared about her, but he didn't want to get too personal. "I believe God has a good plan for Zack, and I believe I've become involved in this for a reason."

Judge Harrison toyed with the napkin holding the silverware as he deliberated. "Over the years, I've become a pretty good judge of character. Although I don't know this young man you've taken an interest in, I do know enough about you to believe you have good intentions." He fell silent for several moments.

When Aiden couldn't take the suspense anymore, he asked, "So, what do you say?"

"I'll pray about it. After lunch we'll head to the sheriff's office. You'll have my answer then."

~*~

Summer's cellphone rang as she parked at the sheriff's station. She plucked her phone from her purse. Riley's number appeared on the screen. The tension in her shoulders ratcheted up a notch. She'd hoped Aiden would've been on the line. He should've called by now.

She stared at the phone, debating whether to answer. If she explained what was happening without knowing the outcome, Riley would be beside herself with worry. But she couldn't lie to her sister and she couldn't simply ignore the truth. Squeezing her eyes shut, Summer pressed the connect button. "I have something to tell you and I don't want you to freak out."

"What? Is it Zack? What'd he do?" Riley's voice pitched higher with each word. "Is he hurt?"

OK. So maybe she hadn't started out with the most reassuring words. "I can explain. He's not injured. He's in a little bit of trouble, but Aiden's helping out. Zack should be out of jail by the end of the day."

A choked sob followed by a fit of coughing sounded from the cellphone's speaker.

Oh, she'd never make a good bearer of bad news. She simply didn't have the eloquence. "It's not as dire as it sounds." But in some respects, it was. Zack was in jail on her watch. She'd failed miserably and she'd only had Zack under her wing a few days.

"I thought things were going so well. You said he had a great time tubing."

"Yeah, well, turns out before the trip he had a little adventure of his own. He stole some things from my neighbors."

"Which ones?"

"Dr. Paxton and Aiden." Summer's stomach twisted into knots. This was so not the news she'd wanted to give Riley.

"Let me guess? The doctor is pressing charges?"

"Not exactly." Summer explained her similar assumptions and Aiden's plan to help Zack.

Riley remained quiet for a moment, then sighed. "Maybe Aiden has the right idea. Maybe a night in a cell and community service is the wake-up call Zack needs."

Summer's jaw dropped open. "You think so?"

"I've always gotten Zack off the hook and nothing's changed. I thought letting him move to a different location would help. But, if that alone isn't working, maybe he does need something to scare him straight."

Encouraged by Riley's support, Summer perked up. "Aiden grew up around a lot of other kids and has experience with all kinds of personality types. He's good with people from all walks of life."

"So you think he can pull this off? You really think Zack will respond to him?"

Yes. She did. And that proved beyond a doubt that she'd begun to trust Aiden. Isn't that what he'd asked for? Her trust? He'd be delighted to know she'd given it to him. "If anyone can get through to Zack, it's Aiden. He's steady as a rock. He's faithful. Committed—"

"And you are falling in love with him."

Summer choked on her next breath. She took a moment to recover as she twisted her ring. "Maybe I am, but he is a firefighter. Always will be." Nervous energy built and she shoved out of the car.

"So what if he's in a risky job? I told you not to let that stop you from following your heart. I'd hoped you would listen."

Heat sweltered from the pavement and Summer strode toward the front door. "How did we get on the subject of my love life?"

"Because it's been too long since you've had an

interest in anybody. And now that you do, I don't want to see you throw it away because you're afraid of losing him once you've got him."

"You lost your husband."

"Yes, and God is seeing me through."

Summer paused at the door. The nights she'd lain awake beside Riley as she mourned the loss of her husband would forever haunt her. Would she ever stand on solid ground again? "I'm still afraid."

"Promise me you'll give this guy a chance. He's probably already in love with you. Why else would he be helping Zack?"

"In love with me? I doubt it. He rescues people for a living. He's probably helping Zack out of some kind of sense of duty. Or, maybe it's his way of being neighborly."

"I'm not even going to respond to that."

Aiden's truck appeared down the street, heading her way. He drove into the parking lot, followed by an older couple in a full-sized sedan. "I gotta go. Aiden's here. And I think the judge has followed him."

"OK. Let me know how it goes. If Aiden's plan doesn't work, I'll pack my bags and drive there."

"I don't think that'll be necessary. Aiden seems confident that everything will work out." Summer drew in a deep breath. "I'm beginning to think so, too."

30

Less than an hour after entering the sheriff's station, Judge Harrison made his decision. Zack would evade juvenile detention by performing community service at the fire station. Aiden had followed through with his promise, and Summer had a newfound hope for Zack's future.

Summer walked out with Zack while Aiden stayed behind filling out paperwork. She tapped the car's remote and unlocked the doors as she rounded the vehicle. "I hope you appreciate what Aiden's doing for you."

Zack kept his eyes downcast as he kicked a stray pebble across the pavement. "He's the one who pressed the charges to begin with. Now he gets to play the hero to impress you."

Summer fought the irritation bubbling inside. Didn't Zack know how blessed he was? "Aiden had every right to press charges. But he didn't have to keep you out of jail and offer to look after you."

"You're defending him because you like him." Zack plopped into the car.

Summer climbed in next to him, cranked the ignition, and set the air conditioning to high. Ignoring his comment, she suggested, "I think it'll do you good to spend some time with him."

"Why? He's not my dad."

She stiffened. She'd had countless conversations about Doug's passing with Riley, but she'd never delved into the subject with Zack for fear of saying the wrong thing. But now she couldn't afford to let her insecurities rule. "No one can replace your father. I'm not even suggesting that. I just hope you can learn something from all this."

Zack shrugged and slumped in his seat.

Well, this conversation was going nowhere fast. Maybe she should've kept to dog-sitting and left the parenting to Riley. Even when Patches went after Tom cat, he hadn't been this difficult to handle.

Summer shifted the car into drive and pulled onto the road.

Zack kept silent on the way to The Meadows as he looked out the passenger-side window. He leaned against the door and fiddled with the handle as if contemplating an escape.

The brooding teen beside Summer made the miles seem to pass in slow motion. When she thought he wouldn't talk anymore, Zack's leery gaze darted to her.

"Does Mom know about this?"

"Yes."

He scoffed. "I bet you couldn't wait to call her. You two talk about everything."

"We talk about everything because we're sisters." They rounded a curve and the afternoon sun streamed through the windshield. Summer flipped down the visor. "I did wait to tell her until I was already at the sheriff's office to pick you up."

"Is she on her way to get me?"

Summer's heart sank. "Is that what you want? Did you steal so your mom would take you home?"

"No." He shook his head. "I'm not ready to go home yet."

Summer turned into the driveway and slowed as

she considered his words. Had he begun to like it here? Perhaps it had something to do with Kayla. Regardless, it's not like he had a choice now anyway. He'd be arrested again and put in detention if he didn't follow through with his community service.

She maneuvered into the parking lot at The Meadows and shut off the engine. She flexed her stiff fingers—she'd white-knuckled it the entire drive home. "I thought you didn't want to be here."

"That was before." Zack pushed open the door and stepped out.

She wasn't about to let this conversation drop. She followed close behind. "Before what?"

"Never mind." He shoved back hair that refused to stay out of his eyes.

If his reasoning did have something to do with Kayla, why would he have taken her with him to the pawn shop and displayed his thievery? "I really want to know. How about we take a walk?"

"I guess." Zack lifted shoulders that had begun to fill out. Soon enough, he'd be full grown and held accountable for his actions like any other adult. If Zack didn't turn around now, what kind of future would await him? He had such potential, and he could ruin it with one more false move.

Summer cleared her throat to keep her watery eyes from shedding tears. "There's a path that follows the river." She led the way toward a group of cypress trees and flowering bushes, taking the moment to rein in her emotions. She waited until they were on the pathway. "What changed your mind about wanting to stay?"

"I want to hang out with Kayla."

"Thought so. Do you think she'll want to after what happened? She knows you stole those things.

Why did you take her with you to sell them?"

"I don't know. I guess I'm used to my friends thinking stealing is cool. They all do it, too. But Kayla . . . she's different. She looked disappointed in me."

Kayla might be even better for Zack than Summer first assumed. "You can turn this around, you know. It's not too late."

Zack shuffled beside Summer as they walked into a clearing. "If Kayla wanted to, do you think her mom would let me take her out again?" He picked up a rock and tossed it into the river.

"I don't know Marilyn very well, so I couldn't begin to guess. Maybe you can talk with her when you go with Aiden to the fire station. Or better yet, show her you're serious about redeeming yourself. Do what you're supposed to do, and she'll take notice."

"Yeah, right." He scoffed and dipped his head, studying the ground as they passed over the rocky terrain. "No one gets attention for doing the right thing."

"That's not true." Summer stopped mid-step and gently grasped Zack's arm, pulling him to a standstill. "What makes you say that?"

"The only time Mom notices me is when I get in trouble."

Summer's senses went on high alert. "Have you been stealing to get your mom's attention?"

Zack averted his gaze so fast Summer didn't get the chance to read his expression. Every fiber of her being screamed that she'd nailed it. It made sense. What better way to garner a captive audience than to stir up trouble? So, she'd uncovered the root of the problem. Maybe she wasn't so bad at this parenting thing after all. "I know she works more hours than she did before, but I also know she would do anything for you."

Riley had always kept her family top priority.

"She's different now." Zack shook his head and continued walking.

Summer leapt forward to keep up. "Talk to me. What's different about her?"

"She pretends all the time like everything is OK. But I still hear her crying at night. She shelters me as if I can't deal with what happened. She won't be real with me." His voice cracked, and for a moment, he sounded like the vulnerable boy she used to know. "It's like she has shut me out to protect me, but that's not what I want."

Summer wrapped an arm around his shoulder, and to her relief, he didn't pull away. "Have you told her how you feel?"

"Why should I? She's too wrapped up in trying to act as if everything is normal." After a few more steps, he met her gaze again, his expression wary. "So, you gonna tell Mom about this?"

"No, Zack. You are."

He lifted his brows, and although he kept walking, he might as well have dug in his heels. "You gonna make me?" He edged out of her grasp.

"I won't have to. Sooner or later, you'll figure out that telling her how you feel is a better option than keeping doing what you've been doing. You might be surprised at how things will change."

"Like you're the expert at relationships." Zack slanted a sideways glance her way. "Last I heard, Aiden was still waiting to know how you feel about him. You love him. Why don't you tell him?"

31

"Well, Patches, things are certainly easier said than done." Summer snuggled with the dog as she settled onto a chair on her balcony. The warm evening breeze carried floral scents from Dottie's growing population of potted flowers. Summer closed her eyes and inhaled the sweet fragrance.

If only life could remain as simple as communing with nature and soaking up sunshine. But circumstances had a tendency to sabotage her attempts at total relaxation. A week after her talk with Zack, he'd yet to tell his mother how he felt, and Summer fought the urge to spill the news. Zack needed to come forward on his own, and she prayed he would, given enough time.

She hadn't told Aiden she was falling for him either, but that was different. She hadn't made her decision yet. Why let him know how deeply she cared for him if she wasn't going to pursue a relationship? It would only confuse matters.

Although she'd thought about Aiden often, he had kept Zack busy, and she'd seen little of both of them. Loneliness had crept in a time or two, but she didn't allow it to linger. Spending time with a male role model was what Zack needed. She wouldn't get in the way.

"At least I have you, Patches." She ran her hands along the length of his back.

He wagged his tail and then rested his head on her

lap.

"What's the matter? Do you miss Zoe?" According to Dottie, Patches and Zoe had become inseparable. Devin even let Dottie keep Zoe during the day sometimes so the two dogs could play.

A round of barking sounded from below and Patches perked up his ears.

Summer glanced over the railing as Devin tossed a ball across the yard. Zoe ran after it, her little legs pumping as fast and hard as she could manage. Summer stood and Patches spotted Zoe. He squirmed and whined, trying to get out of her hands. She hadn't spoken with Devin since the encounter at the sheriff's office, and she hoped he hadn't held a grudge against her or Zack.

"Patches wants to play, too," Summer announced. "Would you mind if we joined you?"

Devin looked up and his wide, easy smile indicated he welcomed the idea. "We'd love the company."

Summer headed inside and then down the stairs. By the time she reached the foyer, Patches had jumped from her arms and beat her to the door. Once outside, the dogs ran toward each other and sniffed a greeting.

Devin's smile remained in place. He wore a pair of jeans and a collared shirt, the most casual she'd seen him since he'd moved in. He nodded toward Patches. "Dog-sitting again?"

Summer sauntered toward him. "Dottie has more of a social life than I do."

"I could help with that." Devin winked.

"Sorry. Still not interested."

"I appreciate a woman who can be direct." Admiration sparked in his gaze.

"So, does that mean there are no hard feelings with what happened with Zack?"

"As long as nothing else happens, we're good."

Summer's tension eased. "Aiden's been working with Zack. You won't have any more trouble." She hoped. According to reports from Aiden, Zack had done everything that was asked of him at the station, with little complaint. Aiden had suggested Zack's motivation relied heavily on impressing Kayla's mother so he could regain her approval, but Summer didn't mind so much. She'd welcome anything that kept Zack on the straight and narrow.

The fire department had scheduled a visit to Hope Haven Children's Home today, and Summer was anxious to hear how that had turned out.

Aiden promised a full report, and he should be calling soon.

Devin cleared his throat. "While we're clearing the air, I know we talked about this before, but I want to make certain you understand that I didn't mean to come across as a loser when I gave you those roses and then took off at the mention of your nephew."

"Don't worry about it. I'd almost forgotten about it." In fact, she'd tossed the now-wilted roses into the trash and pressed the flower Aiden had given her between pages of a book. Once dried, she'd store the keepsake somewhere safe. Call it sentimental, but that little flower meant a lot.

"I just didn't want to give you the wrong impression." Devin picked up the ball and tossed it again.

Patches and Zoe bounded across the yard after it.

"Has your ankle fully healed from Zoe's nip?"

Only a couple of pink areas remained. The small

scarring seemed trivial compared to the car accident she'd endured. Although she'd physically recovered from both incidences, she occasionally had nightmares about rabid Chihuahuas attacking her inside a car as it tumbled down a ravine. "It's fine now."

"Good. Zoe's a little high-strung, but I don't think she'll hurt you again." The little dog ran between Summer's feet while playing a game of chase with Patches. "See, she didn't draw blood this time."

"That's a good sign." Summer grinned.

Dr. Devin Paxton wasn't that bad of a guy. And his dog...well, just because Zoe didn't launch an attack didn't mean Summer would be cuddling with her any time soon.

Summer's cellphone rang. Aiden. Finally. "Excuse me for a moment, Devin." She took a step back and answered. "Hey. I was hoping to hear from you. How'd things go at Hope Haven?"

"Really well." The rich timbre of his voice soothed. "I think Zack has realized how good he's got it now that he's interacted with kids who've lost both parents." His voice became muffled. "Isn't that right, Zack?"

Zack replied, but Summer couldn't decipher the words.

"Thank you so much for doing this for him," she said.

"I'm doing it for you, too."

Summer warmed from the inside out.

Patches and Zoe tangled with each other, play fighting. Their sudden growls turned into a barking frenzy.

"What's going on?" Aiden asked.

"Patches and Zoe are having a play date in the

yard." Summer eased a bit farther away.

"Ah. I see. I suppose Paxton's there too. Is he behaving?"

"Why? Jealous?"

"Should I be?"

"Not at all. I turned him down flat this time."

"He asked you out again? I'm going to have to put a ring on your finger and set that guy straight."

Summer choked on her next breath. She swallowed. Hard. Her palms broke into a sweat and her nerve endings tingled. He couldn't be serious, could he? A part of her wished he was being serious, and that scared her more than anything.

"Summer? Are you still there?"

"Y-yes. Are you almost home?"

"Heading that way. I thought I'd stop off and grab some dinner for us so no one has to cook tonight. Zack and I vote for Chinese. Sound good?"

Sounded like a date, but she wouldn't point that out. "I love Chinese."

"Great. We'll catch up while we eat. I know I haven't been home much." His tone lowered. "I've missed you."

"I've missed you too."

Kissing noises sounded over the line and then Zack's teasing came across faint. "Summer and Aiden sitting in a tree—"

"All right, now. That's enough." Aiden cut him off.

"Aww. Just when he was getting to the good part." Summer clamped her mouth shut. She shouldn't flirt like this, but it was so much fun.

Devin cast a curious glance her way but kept his distance as the dogs continued to play.

"Don't worry." Aiden's voice held a raspy quality. "If you want, there will be plenty of time for the K-I-S-S-I-N-G later."

Oh, she wanted. But would there be ample time? On any given day, Aiden could go in to work and not make it back. With that sobering thought, she reined in her emotions. Letting Aiden into her heart could spell T-R-O-U-B-L-E with a capital *T*.

32

Aiden meant what he'd said about kissing Summer again. But the timing had to be right. Aside from occasional flirtations, he kept his interactions with her on a friendship level for the next couple of weeks, all the while praying she would face her fears and give this thing between them a chance.

As he flipped through TV channels on an overcast Sunday afternoon, his mind kept straying toward her. With his thoughts focused on his lovely neighbor, it took the warning signal from the National Weather Service a moment to register.

As words came across in a computer-like digital voice, Aiden sat up straight. He edged forward and turned up the volume.

A flood warning had been issued for Glade Springs and all the surrounding counties. The light drizzle coming down outside didn't seem enough to account for a flash flood, but that didn't mean the rain farther upriver wasn't soaking mountainsides and swelling tributaries. Statistics had proven the likelihood of drowning increased in high waters.

Summer could've been one of those numbers when she'd ventured too far on the river, and again when her vehicle had tumbled into the overflowing stream. She hadn't gone out on the river today, had she?

Tossing aside the remote, Aiden pulled a T-shirt over his head and strode across the hall. "Summer?"

He knocked. Perhaps he was being a little overprotective, but still...

The door opened. Summer stood with hair secured into a ponytail, a feather duster in hand. "Oh, hey. I was just doing a little cleaning. Everything OK?"

Aiden's worry deflated. "It is now. I came over because the National Weather Service has issued a flash-flood warning. I wanted to make sure you weren't anywhere near the water." He took a step back. "I'll let you get back to what you were doing."

"Flash flood? The storms were supposed to be coming in later tonight."

"Apparently, they moved in faster than expected. And to make matters worse, they've stalled over the mountains. With this new influx of rain, the water could rise to dangerous levels within the next hour or two."

Summer's eyes widened. "Marilyn called earlier. She finally gave Zack permission to take Kayla out again. They had such a good time tubing before they decided to go again."

"In that case we don't need to worry. The owners of River Run Outfitters watch the weather closely. If there's even a chance of dangerous water levels, they cancel the trips. Maybe Zack and Kayla will end up seeing a movie or something."

Summer's concerned features didn't relax. If anything, her pinched brows drew together tighter. "They weren't going on a group tour. Zack and Kayla went with Robbie and Stuart. They took their own inner tubes."

Aiden's muscles constricted. "Are they wearing lifejackets?"

"They're supposed to be." Summer's coloring

faded to sheer white. "But you know teenagers. They don't always do what they're told."

"Where did they put in at?"

"A little north of Glade Springs at the boat landing on Route 234."

"At least we have a starting point." Aiden headed for the door. "We need to find them."

"I could try calling Zack." Summer fished her cellphone from her purse. Then she hesitated. "He wouldn't have taken his phone on the river. We have to get going and find them before it's too late." She grabbed her keys, fumbled, and dropped them.

Aiden scooped up the keys and placed them in her hand. "It would be better if we split up. I'll check the boat landing first. You can stop by the access points along River Road." He stepped close, making sure to drive home his point. "If you see them, call me. Whatever you do, do *not* go in the water."

~*~

Summer checked several areas without luck. On the fifth stop, desperation set in. Tree limbs and other debris passed along the river at an alarming rate. The rain had to be coming down in torrents somewhere upriver. The muddied water held such power, anyone unfortunate enough to be caught in it would be helpless against the current.

Summer's cellphone rang and she peeled her gaze from the river long enough to check the caller ID. Aiden's name appeared. "Did you find them?" She skipped any normal greeting—this wasn't a normal day.

"We have a situation." Aiden sounded breathless.

Her heart plummeted. "What's happening? Where are you?"

"I'm at the boat ramp off of Route 234. We've got two in the water."

"Zack? Is he...?" Summer ran toward the car.

"He's been overtaken by the current. He's hanging on to a limb. We're trying to reach him."

Lord, give him strength to hold on.

She slid into the driver's seat and started the engine. "I'll be right there."

Time seemed to stand still as she drove. As if on autopilot, she took the curves without thought. She passed slower cars when possible, her mind focused on reaching her destination. What was happening? Aiden had said Zack was in the water. Where was Kayla? What about Robbie and Stuart?

By the time she arrived at the ramp, an assortment of vehicles surrounded the area, including two sheriff's patrol cars, the fire department's ladder truck, a couple of Virginia Department of Game and Inland Fisheries SUVs, and Virginia State Police sedans.

Summer parked on the roadside and weaved her way to the river.

Shouts and commands from first responders covered the area, engines roared, and lights flashed.

But everything faded as her gaze landed on Zack. He bobbed in the water, clinging onto a branch with one arm and a black inner tube with the other as the current levied against him.

Kayla floundered about thirty-five yards upriver from him. Kayla had no inner tube and no hold on a branch.

Lord, help them . . .

The current swept Kayla toward Zack, but he

would have to release his lifesaving hold on the branch to catch her.

Summer's knees weakened. She stepped along the shoreline parallel to the struggling teens. "Zack!" He seemed so close. Yet, with the river flowing between them, they might as well have been worlds apart. "Hold on."

Zack extended an arm when Kayla drew near, but the powerful water forced Kayla past him. He let go of the branch and tumbled downriver after her.

"No." Acting on pure instinct, Summer lunged forward, stepping into the cool river. Her sandals slid on moss-covered rocks and she lost her balance. As she started falling, a strong arm clamped around her waist, hauling her back.

"You can't go in after them," Aiden shouted.

She clawed his arms. "I have to help."

"You can't." His warning came harsh and resolute. "Not from here. If you get in the water, we'll be rescuing three people instead of two."

"What happened to Robbie and Stuart?"

"They're fine. They never got in. They saw Zack and Kayla in trouble and called 911." Aiden set Summer on shore, keeping his iron grip intact. "I need to go after them. But I won't release you until I know you're not going to end up another victim."

The longer she struggled, the less help Zack and Kayla would get. "Don't worry about me." She forced herself to go limp in Aiden's arms. "Save them."

Aiden let her go. "Stay away from the water." With one last warning glance, he jogged away.

Summer kept watch on the river as she forced herself to retreat.

Zack managed to grab hold of Kayla, and she

grasped the inner tube. But how long could they hang on? Debris clouded the water, and mud masked hidden dangers beneath. Zack latched on to another overhanging branch, slowing their movements long enough for shore-bound rescuers to toss lines.

But the desperate attempts failed. Firefighters extended a ladder from the truck, but the rungs didn't reach far enough.

The current grew stronger by the minute as the water level continued to rise.

Summer paced. Prayed. And paced some more.

A crack sounded as the limb Zack held on to split in two, sending the pair careening downriver once again.

"The boat's here," someone shouted above the organized chaos as a rescue boat motored close and pulled to shore. Aiden climbed on board.

Kayla let out a terrified scream as she slipped from the inner tube. She fought to stay above the surface, but her efforts were in vain—the water swallowed her again.

"Kayla." Zack's voice carried above all else.

Kayla resurfaced, Zack grabbed her, and the swollen river took full advantage, dragging them both away.

Refusing to wait by the sidelines, Summer sprinted toward the boat and leapt inside as the driver backed away from shore. She landed hard, skinning her hands and knees, but she ignored the pain as Aiden's gaze zoned in on her.

"What do you think you're doing?" His brows cinched together.

The current caught hold of the boat and swept it away from shore. If he wanted her off, they would lose precious time getting her back on land. "Go." She didn't waste breath defending her actions.

Aiden handed over a lifejacket before securing one on himself. "We'll talk about this later." The intensity in his gaze dared her to defy him.

"Later is good." She'd agree to just about anything to get his focus back to Zack and Kayla. "They're almost out of sight." She pointed toward the struggling teens as she snapped on the life preserver.

Aiden nodded at the driver. "Let's go get them."

The young man jammed the throttle forward and the motor roared above the sound of the raging river.

Aiden prepared a rescue line, his practiced movements showing expertise. As they caught up to the teens, he widened his stance. He tossed the line.

Zack managed to grab hold and fasten it around Kayla's torso, but somewhere in the process, Zack lost hold of the inner tube and slipped under the water. Bubbles erupted, swirled, disappeared. Churned-up water concealed any sign of him.

"Zack. No." Breathless, Summer scrambled to the side.

Aiden hauled Kayla toward the boat and hefted her inside.

Tears streamed down Kayla's face. "Zack..."

"I'll get him." Aiden knelt before the girl. "I need you to stay seated. Got it?"

She nodded, shivering from head to toe.

Summer scanned the river. Still no sign of Zack. "He's not coming up."

Aiden stood, preparing to do...something. Summer wasn't sure what. He climbed up front. "Over there." He pointed toward a series of rapids where whitewater bumped over hidden rocks.

"I don't see him." Summer edged her way to the front.

Aiden jumped in feet first. He disappeared and then bobbed above the surface amongst a mass of broken branches. He disentangled himself and swam toward the rapids. In spite of the life preserver fighting to hold him above water, Aiden ducked under. Moments later, he emerged with Zack in tow.

Summer breathed a tremendous sigh of relief as Zack coughed and sputtered, gaining his bearings.

"Relax. I've got you." Aiden's reassuring words carried across the distance as he tugged Zack toward the boat.

Kayla and Summer helped Zack climb inside. He landed with a thump, breathing hard.

Summer took Zack into her arms, and water saturated her clothes. "I thought I was going to lose you."

"I'm all right." Zack shoved at her, a blush staining his cheeks as he glanced at Kayla.

Oh, yeah. The whole hugging thing was so not cool in front of a girlfriend. At least he was still alive to be embarrassed. Summer edged away, scanning his bumps and bruises. Cuts on his arm bled and his hands shook, but all things considered, he looked in good shape.

Summer leveled her gaze on his. "I think it's about time you gave your mom a call and got things straight between you two, don't you?"

Zack nodded. "I almost lost the chance to tell her...It could've been too late." His voice cracked and tears glistened.

Summer held back tears of her own—the time for Zack's healing had begun. "You'll be OK. You know that, right?"

Zack nodded, and then Kayla launched herself into Zack's arms, sobbing.

He soothed a hand along her back and held tight.

It was just as well. Summer had Aiden to look after. She leaned over and found him grasping the boat's side. She beamed a smile his way. All reservations aside, she just wanted to get her hands on him. "Climb in here and let me thank you properly." It was time for that K-I-S-S-I-N-G he'd spoken about.

"I like the sound of that." He returned her victorious grin.

Summer held out a helping hand, but then an object—approaching fast—caught her attention. A broken branch about a foot in diameter speared toward Aiden, propelled by the cruel current. "Look out!"

He twisted around. But it was too late—the limb's jagged edge plowed into Aiden's temple. Blood gushed and Summer screamed.

Aiden's grip slipped from the boat as his eyes closed, the current forcing him face down as it carried him away.

33

Ignoring the driver's warning for her to stay in the boat, Summer scrambled over the side and splashed into the swift water, paddling, clawing her way toward Aiden. But each time she neared him, the river split them apart again. The driver circled, saying something, but she couldn't hear above the river's rage. She didn't care. She had one goal; she had to reach Aiden.

His limp body remained defenseless to surrounding forces. Debris battered exposed skin. Water beat against his submerged face and blood tinged the water a dull pink around his head.

Bile rose in Summer's throat. She'd asked Aiden for time to make her decision. Now, time had become her enemy. How long could he survive without oxygen? Was it already too late to save him? She swam harder, faster.

Her useless fears had stolen several weeks that they could've been together. She wanted that precious time back. But it was gone, never to be relived. Regret sliced through her, and understanding swept over her as fast and swift as the current—fears had robbed her of too much, for too long.

Never again.

Lord, let him live. I need him. I want him in my life. Please give me another chance to make this right.

Summer stroked her arms through the water, fighting for Aiden and for the life she so desperately wanted. She surged forward, drawing closer. Her fingers grazed his lifejacket once. Twice. Then, on the third try, she managed to grab hold of the top strap. She flipped him over, exposing his face to life-sustaining oxygen.

The rescue boat rumbled alongside them, and the driver hefted Aiden from the river first, and then Summer next. She fell to her knees beside Aiden as he lay prone on the boat's deck.

"Breathe," she demanded.

Lord, You have taught us the thief comes only to steal and kill and destroy. You came to us so we may have life and have it in abundance. I am claiming that promise. I want to live life to the fullest with Aiden. Forgive me for allowing fears to rule my decisions and please let it not be too late.

Cushioning Aiden's head with a hand, Summer leaned in to give him mouth-to-mouth.

Aiden stirred beneath her touch. "Does this mean you've made up your mind?" he rasped as his hand curled around the nape of her neck. His lips moved against hers in a kiss so startling her entire world narrowed until only Aiden remained.

Relief washed away pent-up anxiety.

God was giving them a second chance.

Summer eased away and sat upright, taking in Aiden's pale features.

Blood trickled from the gash on his temple, seeping into his hair. Various bruises formed on his skin, but even so, he'd never looked so tempting.

"You almost drowned. You're bleeding. And you want to know if I'll date you?"

"Now's as good a time as any to ask." He grinned, wincing as if the slight movement pained him.

"In that case...yes. I want to date you." And so much more...

The driver handed over a gauze pad, and Summer pressed it to Aiden's wound.

Aiden covered her hand with his as his expression sobered, his sapphire eyes growing intense. "And if something like this happens again? Or even something worse? Something I didn't survive. Would you have any regrets?"

"I already have regrets."

Aiden took in a slow breath, disappointment registering. "Then this won't work. I am who God has created me to be. That won't change because I've fallen in love with you."

Tears she'd been holding back escaped in full force. He loved her. Her spirits soared. Her heart pounded, but best of all, her hopes exploded. "I don't want you to change. I love you for who you are. As you are."

A spark of anticipation lit in his eyes, but caution remained evident. "Then what do you regret?"

She smoothed a hand along his face, cautious to keep pressure on the cloth covering his wound. "I regret the time we've already lost. I would rather have one day with you than spend the rest of my life wondering what could've been."

Aiden's strained features softened into a smile. "In that case, we'd better get started." He pressed his lips to hers, conveying a promise of much more to come.

After a few moments, Summer eased away and looked into Aiden's expectant eyes. "We're doing this all wrong."

"What do you mean?" He glanced at her lips as if the kiss had been ineffectual, which was so not the case—her entire being responded to his touch as if he was meant to start fires, not extinguish them.

Summer cleared her throat and smiled. "I was supposed to officially welcome you to The Meadows before we became a couple."

"We were also supposed to date before we fell in love." Aiden shrugged. "But I guess stranger things have happened."

Very true. Stranger things *had* happened. And it all started with an ill-fated blackberry cobbler, a cherished Chihuahua named Patches, and a mischievous Tom cat.

I trust You, Lord. I trust You with Aiden and I trust You with my future. Thank You for the second chance…but most of all, thank You for changing my heart.

Editor's Note

When we decided to dedicate the proceeds of a book to charity, there were a few things to consider: who would write the book, what the book would be about, and which charity would receive the proceeds.

All three answers came easy: Wendy Davy is a talented author whose books are loved by readers everywhere, and she's been a blessing to Pelican Book Group for many years. When she pitched the firefighter storyline, we were overjoyed. What better subject for a book dedicated to charitable contribution than a hero who dedicates his life to saving others? But like so many everyday heroes, Aiden not only rescues people from burning buildings, but also cares about his neighbours in special and personal ways. Anyone who is marginalized or disadvantaged or going down a wrong path, Aiden tries to help.

Just as Aiden in our story, we wanted to donate to a charity that served people in many ways. One charity rose to the top of the list because of its diverse activities. Food for the Poor® provides food, housing, health care, education, water, emergency relief, and micro-enterprise assistance; and with less than 5 percent of donations being used for administrative costs, we could be confident that our donation would actually support these projects. (To learn more about Food for the Poor®, visit www.foodforthepoor.org.)

Thank you for purchasing this book. Rest assured your donation will enrich the lives of many. Please encourage a friend to purchase a copy of this book. Together, we can save lives.

God bless you,
Nicola Martinez, Editor-in-Chief

Thank You

We appreciate you reading this White Rose Publishing title. For other inspirational stories, please visit our on-line bookstore at www.pelicanbookgroup.com.

For questions or more information, contact us at customer@pelicanbookgroup.com.

White Rose Publishing
Where Faith is the Cornerstone of Love™
an imprint of Pelican Ventures Book Group
www.PelicanBookGroup.com

Connect with Us
www.facebook.com/Pelicanbookgroup
www.twitter.com/pelicanbookgrp

To receive news and specials, subscribe to our bulletin
http://pelink.us/bulletin

May God's glory shine through
this inspirational work of fiction.

AMDG

Free Book Offer

We're looking for booklovers like you to partner with us! Join our team of influencers today and receive at least one free eBook per month. Maybe more!

For more information
Visit http://pelicanbookgroup.com/booklovers
or e-mail
booklovers@pelicanbookgroup.com.